Praise for Shiloh Walker's *Beautiful Girl*

"Just beautiful."

~ *Karen KarenKnowsBest.com*

"…packs quite a punch…this story is one of the best I have read so far this year."

~ *Kate Garrabrant, RRTErotic.com*

"…this is one good read where I am concerned."

~ *Mrs. Giggles, MrsGiggles.com*

"…an exceptional story that will touch every emotion…I can't recommend this story enough."

~ *Lisa Freeman The Romance Studio*

Look for these titles by *Shiloh Walker*

Now Available

The Hunters Series:
The Huntress
Hunter's Pride
Malachi
Legends: Hunters and Heroes
Hunter's Edge

Always Yours
Talking with the Dead
Playing for Keeps
For the Love of Jazz
Vicious Vixen

Beautiful Girl

Shiloh Walker

A Samhain Publishing, Ltd. publication.

Samhain Publishing, Ltd.
577 Mulberry Street, Suite 1520
Macon, GA 31201
www.samhainpublishing.com

Beautiful Girl
Copyright © 2009 by Shiloh Walker
Print ISBN: 978-1-59998-989-1
Digital ISBN: 1-59998-873-9

Editing by Heidi Moore
Cover by Scott Carpenter

First Samhain Publishing, Ltd. electronic publication: January 2008
First Samhain Publishing, Ltd. print publication: May 2009

Chapter One

Coming home was both heaven and hell. Delilah Prescott pulled her beat up Corolla off the two lane highway, right in front of the welcome sign. *Welcome to Prescott, Tennessee—Small Town, Big Heart.* Located in the mostly rural county of Pike near the Tennessee/Kentucky border, the town's main claim to fame was that Daniel Boone had spent some time in the general area.

It was a nice little town, though. Just about everybody knew each other and even strangers were made to feel welcome. Lots of strangers, especially on weekends and in the summer. Just south of Lake Cumberland, Prescott was a stopping point, watering hole and overnight lodging for all the families that flocked to the lake that didn't want to stay at the campground but didn't have the money for the rental cabins.

The lake was a popular vacation spot during the hot months of July and August. Over the past twenty years or so, Prescott had become something of an antique mecca. The result was tourist coming through the small town on a regular basis. Small shops lined Main Street and from what she could tell, some of the retail prosperity had spread out past the immediate area of downtown.

She saw what looked like a for real steakhouse. Not just the diner or Lula's Café. A real restaurant, complete with neon sign. She wondered what else had changed in the past twelve years.

Besides her, of course.

"God." Del closed her eyes and prayed she had the strength to do this. Divine intervention was the only thing that had given her the strength to come down here and judging from the watery state of her knees, she was going to need a lot more divine help to keep from jumping back in the car and leaving as fast as she could.

But she couldn't keep running. She was tired of it.

Besides, she'd made herself a promise and she was going to keep it. She was going to kill the one person she'd kept in contact with. Not very frequent contact, but enough that the bastard knew where to find her. Vance Prescott was her cousin, and she loved him dearly, but she was going to kill him for passing her address on to Manda Jones. If he hadn't shared her address with her old school friend, then Del wouldn't have been standing here dealing with this dilemma.

For years, she hadn't talked to anybody from her childhood home but then she'd run into Vance in Cincinnati. They'd spent a couple hours talking—not about what had sent Del running. The one friend that Del had told was dead, and Del wasn't interested in sharing her miserable history with anybody else.

But they'd talked. Just about things. Old friends. Life. Vance was a teacher at the county high school now. Sounded like he was good at it too. He definitely seemed to enjoy his job.

A pity, because she was still going to kill him. The only reason she'd given him any contact information was because Vance had deduced just why she didn't want to give it to him. *I won't share it with anybody—definitely not your mom. I just want to keep in contact.*

So she had given it to him. Del wanted no contact, *none*, with the ice-cold woman who had given birth to her. There was no chance in hell that Louisa had changed and even if she had, the sense of betrayal, shame and outrage wouldn't let Del forgive what the woman had done to her.

"Stop dragging your feet," she muttered. "This probably won't be too bad." Del had missed home. No matter that she had made a life for herself in Cincinnati, no matter that she was making a difference there, Prescott was home.

She'd even enjoyed her short emails back and forth with Manda. Manda was one person who definitely hadn't changed, at least not much. Her best friend from childhood still didn't know how to accept *no* for an answer. It was time for the 10 year reunion for the graduating class of Pike County High School, 1997. Manda headed up the reunion committee and she wanted Delilah there.

Manda hadn't listened to Del when she pointed out, "I didn't graduate with you, Manda."

"Oh, since when did that matter? Come on, honey... I miss you."

Those simple words had put a knot in Del's throat. She missed Manda. She missed home. And Blake... Del turned away from the welcome sign. She wasn't going to think about Blake Mitchell. Wouldn't do her any good. As she circled the car, she realized she was literally dragging her feet. Resolutely, she straightened her shoulders and forced down the dread sliding inside her.

She wasn't a kid anymore. Whatever came flying at her this time, she could handle.

Del took a deep, steadying breath. "Let's get this over with," she muttered. With an automatic, absent gesture, she flipped her braids back over her shoulders before putting the car back into drive. She checked the rearview mirror and pulled back onto the highway.

A glance at the clock on the dashboard told her she still had a good hour to kill before she was supposed to meet Manda at the diner. Manda had wanted to meet at Lula's but it was Wednesday. The entire time Del was growing up, her mother had afternoon tea with the Ladies' Group at Lula's, every Wednesday, like clockwork.

There was no way in hell that Del was ready to see her mother. Matter of fact, she'd be happy to go the entire time without that particular event taking place.

Instead of heading toward the diner, she drove up High Street until she reached Main. A left turn took her into the small heart of Prescott and she couldn't help but smile a little as she saw the old courthouse. The town square looked the same. The big statue of Daniel Boone was still surrounded by a riot of color, flowers that the Ladies maintained. Well, *money* from the Ladies. The Ladies were the well-to-do women of Pike County and most of them wouldn't dare soil their hands, even if it was to plant flowers.

The ice cream parlor was still there, the pink and white striped awning fluttering in the hot afternoon breeze. It was busy, young and old, gathering inside and taking up the little bitty tables in front of the windows. Across the street, on the courthouse grounds, were more tables, larger picnic tables that had teenaged kids sitting on the benches or the table surface itself.

A faint smile curved her lips. She could remember hot summer nights spent cruising around the square, holding Blake Mitchell's hand in one of hers, and the other hand holding an ice cream cone. Double Chocolate Swirl, her favorite, from Macy's Dairy Barn. Afternoons spent down at the lake.

Late one hot summer night, she had spent some very hot and heavy minutes with Blake on a table in the Square, on one of those very tables. They'd made out, gotten themselves so worked up, they just might have gone all the way, right there in the open, if Blake's older brother hadn't come driving up. She wondered if Travis was still the sheriff.

Travis was fifteen years older than Blake. Del had adored him. He was funny, kind and he always treated her like a kid sister. She'd asked herself a million times what would have happened if she'd gone to him. Instead

11

of running. He would have believed her. Looking back now, she knew that. He would have believed her and her entire life might have been different.

"Don't go there, Del," she whispered. Propping her elbow on the car door, she rested her cheek against her palm. The light in front of her changed, but she didn't notice until the old guy in the pickup behind her honked his horn. She waved in apology and pulled over. Driving around probably wasn't the best idea. At least not until she could get all the memories crowding her head under control.

"I should have waited until Friday. Or not come at all," she mumbled as a heavy ball of nausea started to churn inside her gut. She climbed out of the car and stared across the street at Lula's. Two o'clock. Right on time to see that the Ladies did indeed still meet for afternoon tea. She could see them all filing inside, laughing and talking to one another, wearing pretty pastels and soft whites, their hair fixed to perfection. Although she wasn't close enough to see, she'd knew they'd all be wearing their make up perfectly and their clothes would be accented with just the right amount of jewelry.

The Ladies took themselves quite seriously.

Del turned away from the café. She hadn't seen her mother and she didn't want to.

Behind her was Bess's Bookstore. Faintly, she smiled and then the smile grew until it was a full-out, happy grin. Before high school, before Blake, Bess's had been her favorite place in the whole world. She wondered if Bess was still around. Ducking her head through the driver's window, Del snagged the strap of her small messenger-bag purse. She pulled the strap over her head and settled the purse against her hip, automatically covering it with her hand. Nobody was going to try and lift her purse here, but old habits died hard.

The scent of books, cinnamon and coffee flooded her senses. And when the old woman behind the counter lifted her head and smiled in her direction, Del decided the idea hadn't been a total disaster.

လ

"I still can't get over how different you look," Manda mused. She was quiet for a minute, a rare occurrence, as she sipped her coffee and studied Del. The pretty, freckle-faced redhead looked around. Over the past hour and a half, the diner had emptied out and even the guy at the counter had quit paying so much attention to them and gone out front for a smoke break.

They were completely alone and Del felt her stomach knot as Manda lowered the coffee cup and pinned her with a hard look. "So are you going to tell me what happened? Why you left? Where you went?"

Del shifted around in the padded booth and tried to figure out what to say. She'd known that Manda would ask. As would others. And she had no idea what to say. "Does it really matter? After twelve years?"

Manda looked down at her hands. She had a big, shiny rock on her left hand. She'd ended up marrying somebody from outside of Pike County, a doctor. He'd set up a family practice just off of Main Street, so Prescott actually had two doctors now. Talk about metropolitan, Del thought with a smirk.

"Your mom said she sent you off to a private school up north," Manda said. Although her voice didn't change, there was a flicker of doubt in her eyes. "Is that where you went?"

Del licked her lips, uncertain what to say. She'd wondered what story Louisa Prescott Sanders had concocted to explain away her daughter's sudden disappearance.

Manda reached over and covered Del's hand, squeezing gently. "You weren't at some ritzy private school, were you?"

Del turned her hand over and linked her fingers with Manda's. "Hard to believe that people thought you were the airhead of our bunch," she said, forcing herself to smile.

"What happened, Dee? What happened with you? I mean, I expected you would look a little different. Shoot, I was even prepared to be mad at you, or not like you, taking off like that. You never wrote. You never called. Never came home for holidays. Part of me didn't *want* to like you. But I know you." Manda smiled, but it was a sad one. "We've been friends practically since we were in diapers. Something happened and I want to know what."

ᘛᘚ

The pampered princess of Pike County was back. Delilah Prescott, junior homecoming queen, had been the most beautiful girl in town and she came from one of the richest families in the county, if not the richest. Her family owned half the land in the area and had for going back more than a century.

She'd also been the love of his teenage years, the subject of more wet dreams than he could remember— and the first and only woman to break his heart.

Blake hadn't seen Delilah yet, but everybody seemed to be humming about her return. He'd heard at least ten different times that his old girlfriend was back in town, and had seriously changed over the past twelve years.

Blake glanced in the mirror and smirked a little. Had she changed as much as he had? He smoothed a hand over the gleaming surface of his bald head before grabbing the black Bandana and covering his scalp with it. It had been five years since he'd finished chemo and radiation treatments and the doctors had diagnosed a complete recovery from the Hodgkin's Disease. Blake had more or less accepted his hair wasn't coming back.

As long as the cancer didn't come back, then Blake could deal with the lack of hair just fine. Pretty damn easy, too, considering he was alive and he felt good. There was no more weakness and nagging exhaustion he'd written off as a bad flu bug, hangover, a hundred other insignificant things. Blake had been in a car wreck and his trip to the ER had saved his life. Something weird showed up in his blood count and instead of being checked out for a concussion and broken ribs, he was admitted for what seemed like two thousand tests.

Weird, all it took was one second to change a man forever. He went from being young and living hard to a full and complete stop. He could have died. He'd ignored the little nagging symptoms for too long and by the time the doctors caught it, he was in Stage III.

Blake was lucky, though. He'd had an entire town praying for him, hoping he'd come through and his own stubbornness. He hadn't been ready to die, not at twenty-one. Even through the years of treatment that followed and he was so sick from the chemo, his desperation hadn't ever gotten to the point that he had been ready to quit fighting.

If it wasn't for the bald head, he could almost pretend those few years hadn't happened. Well, if he wanted to. He didn't want to forget. Nothing will change your life quite like the words, *It's cancer.* A man hears those words and it will do some serious things to him. The years spent in hospitals, all the treatments and all the tests, made a guy reevaluate everything.

It also made him grow up—real fast.

Yeah, he'd changed. He was pretty damn sure that Delilah couldn't have changed nearly as much as he had. The first two years after she'd left town, he'd run wild, getting into so much trouble it was a miracle his brother hadn't killed him. Poor Travis had hauled him into jail a dozen times and threatened to throw away the key more than once.

Almost flunking out of high school, barely eking through the first couple years of college, sometimes Blake wondered if it was another miracle that he'd even lived long enough for the Hodgkin's to start trying to kill him. Those first two years of college were just a haze of nonstop parties and last minute cram sessions so he could just scrape by with a passing grade. If he hadn't wanted to come home and see that disappointment in Mom's eyes, he wouldn't have bothered with the cram sessions.

Then he was in that wreck with Douglas Maynard. Doug had been driving, totally plastered. Blake hadn't been too sober himself, but he had lived through the wreck. Doug hadn't. Between watching a friend die right in front of him and surviving cancer, Blake figured he didn't have too much in common with his ex-girlfriend.

Even if he did still dream about her.

As he left his room, he heard the maid talking with his mom's personal nurse, Tammy. Two years ago, Evangeline Mitchell had suffered a series of minor strokes, culminating in a massive one that paralyzed her left side. Tammy Schultz had been with them since they'd brought Evangeline back to Bel Rive from the hospital.

Although the doctors had argued Evangeline might do better in a rehab facility, Blake and his brother knew she needed to be at home. Bel Rive, the Mitchell family estate, had been her home for more than fifty years—It was where she belonged. Hiring the personal nurse had been a compromise, and Tammy had been with them ever since.

Their voices were too low to hear everything, but he heard Delilah's name...and more references about her lunch with Manda at the diner. Exactly how much how Dee changed, he wondered?

Maybe put on fifty pounds and had two or three kids. Oddly enough, that thought didn't really disturb Blake. One of the dreams that bothered him the most was the one where he'd ended up marrying Dee. The dream had them down at the lake in the cabin he'd inherited from his dad and they were making love in the bedroom. From time to time, the dream did change but what usually happened was the sound of a crying baby or a laughing kid interrupted them.

The laughing kid or crying baby didn't bother Blake at all. He wanted kids. As his friends all got married, one by one, he wanted a family more and more, but there just wasn't a woman he was interested in. Except Dee. Even after twelve years, she was the only one he dreamed about. The only woman who could put that ache in his chest when he thought about her too long. Blake hadn't ever gotten over her and he knew it.

So no, thinking about Dee and a couple of kids surrounding her didn't bother him. What bothered him about that mental image was the imagined ring on her left hand. "Shit. You've got to get past this." He finished buttoning his shirt and paused to look in the mirror.

He'd been a deputy with the sheriff's department the past three years. It had taken some time to convince everybody that he wasn't the invalid people wanted to think he was. Not that he looked sick but the Town Council wasn't exactly made up of the most open minded people. Cancer meant a person was sick. Even after he'd been declared cancer free and healthy. That was all there was to it, as far as they were concerned. Convincing them otherwise had taken Blake a while but it had been worth it.

Last year when Travis was voted the town mayor, his deputy Louis Conrad stepped up as sheriff and Blake was now the deputy sheriff. The first few months, he continued wearing the deputy uniform, but eventually, he started wearing a plain white shirt and jeans or khakis, the same as Louis did, the same as Travis had done. He kept his badge on his belt and his weapon under a plain sports coat and that was as good a uniform as any, as far as Blake was concerned.

Normally, he didn't pay his reflection any more attention than necessary, but this time, he lingered. He eyed the black cloth he wore on his head and for the first time in a couple of years, it made him feel self-conscious.

People lost their hair with chemo and radiation. Most of them grew it back. Blake never did. Of course, Travis had been bald by the time he was thirty, so there was a chance Blake would have ended up like this any way. He figured going quick and clean was better than clinging to the illusion of a full head of hair and wasting money on crap that didn't work.

19

But it wasn't just that. Even without the total lack of hair, though, he looked different than he had in high school.

Older. Not just physically. The youth and innocence had been gone a long time but he hadn't really realized just how jaded he looked now. He had put back on the weight he'd lost when he'd had been sick, and then some. He ran religiously and lifted weights, drove forty minutes so he could take Shaolin karate in Hancock three times a week.

After spending years sick and weak, he wasn't ever doing it again so physical fitness was like a religion for him. He hadn't turned into a leaf-eating vegetarian or anything—he wasn't going to take it so seriously that he gave up a good steak or onion rings, but he was careful.

He didn't look bad, he guessed.

Just different.

At least he and Dee would be on equal ground, he figured.

Chapter Two

Something happened and I want to know what, Manda had said.

Something.

Yeah. Something happened, all right. Del wasn't ready to talk about it and she could tell by the look in Manda's eyes that her old friend wasn't buying Del's vague answer, *It's been twelve years. All sorts of somethings have happened.* But, bless her, Manda hadn't pushed.

The subject wasn't closed, though. Far from it. Manda wasn't going to leave it alone. If Del was lucky, though, she'd leave it alone long enough for Del to get through the reunion, to prove to herself she could, and then slip away.

But Del wasn't very convinced things would go her way.

Eight hours after the lunch with Manda, she stood in front of the brightly lit mirror in the guest bathroom. Mrs. Manda Monroe was as stubborn now as she had been in high school. When Del had said she was staying at the little lakeside resort twenty minutes outside of town, Manda had almost thrown a fit. "You'll stay with me." She didn't even ask Del why she didn't go stay at the manor.

When Del tried to argue, Manda had played the ace up her sleeve. "You stay at there and your folks will show up. Louisa can't have her daughter staying at some middle class hotel."

Del's lip curled at the reference to Louisa and her second husband. That was all it would take, and Manda had known it. Even after all these years, Manda knew Del's sore spots.

Del wasn't going to risk having either of them showing up at her door. Manda was one of the few who knew how distant and strained the relationship between Del and Louisa had been and she'd known exactly how to handle Del. When Del reluctantly accepted, Manda had smiled with satisfaction. "I'll even let you watch me send them away," Manda had promised.

But Louisa wouldn't come to Manda's. She wouldn't risk Del airing their personal affairs with an audience. Not considering just how ugly those personal affairs were.

So instead of an impersonal hotel room, Del was standing in the pretty blue and white bathroom and staring at her reflection. Yes. She was different.

She had finally grown her hair out so that it was a little past her shoulders. It was a momentous thing for her. For years, she hadn't been able to stand the feel of it around her shoulders so she'd kept it cropped to chin length. In high school, the butter-yellow curls had fallen to her waist.

He'd used her hair to... Dee moaned as the memories swarmed up, swamping her. *Beautiful little slut—you know you were made for this, weren't you, beautiful girl?* The ugly, hated memories surrounded her, sucking her under. She felt like she was going to drown in them.

Del covered her eyes, as if that would help. It didn't, though. She heard his voice, clear as if he was standing there. *Beautiful girl, my beautiful little bitch, tell me you like it.* She could feel his hands on her, shoving her to her knees and pulling her hair as he made her open her mouth and—

Del whimpered and the high pitched, helpless sound echoed through the bathroom. The sound of it snapped her out of the memory fog and she slapped a hand over her mouth to muffle it. "Shit. Shit. *Shit.*" She turned on the faucet and splashed the icy water on her face. The nausea didn't recede but through sheer will power, she managed to throttle the memories down and she managed to keep from puking.

Barely.

That last night, after William Sanders raped her, she had taken a pair of scissors from the kitchen and chopped her hair off until it was no more than an inch long all over her head. It wasn't enough, though. A few days after she ran away from Prescott, she had bought a box of hair dye and died the choppy blonde strands black.

A few years ago, she'd stopped dyeing it black, settling on a dark, nondescript brown. She didn't look quite so pale and most of the kids she worked with stopped treating her like she was trying to pull a Goth routine just to establish some kind of connection. She straightened it regularly. The natural curls were another reminder of the life she ran away from, the life of Prescott's princess and she hadn't wanted any reminders.

A professional stylist could get rid of the curls and it just took a few regular trips to the salon each year to maintain the razor-straight tresses. She kept her hair braided, she never wore make up and instead of the fun, fashionable clothes she'd once worn, she wore cargo pants or jeans, boots or tennis shoes. And long sleeve shirts. Always long sleeves.

Water dripped from her hands and face as she turned off the water. But instead of straightening up and drying her face off, she remained bent over the sink. Her fingers shook she traced the scar on her left wrist. There was a matching one on her right wrist. Faded now, but she remembered how they had looked when she had first left the hospital ten years ago. It wasn't the first time she'd attempted suicide, but it was the only time she'd come really close.

If that couple hadn't taken a break and pulled their truck over when they did, Del would have bled to death in that little interstate rest stop in Ohio For a very, very long, Del wished that nice lady straight to hell for daring to save her life.

Not now, though. Not even being back here was enough to make her yearn for death. She didn't even want blood. She had come here to see Manda—she missed her old friend. And yes, Del could admit it, she wanted to see Blake and all the friends she'd left behind when she ran away.

She'd come back to prove to herself that she could and she'd come back to face her past. Even though she sincerely didn't want to see her mother, or William, she was going to.

Before she left, Del was going to face Louisa Prescott over what that cold-hearted bitch had allowed to happen—and she'd get answers. Not until Del was ready, though. She'd deal with her mother when she was ready and not a minute before.

Mama, he raped me

The lies you tell, Delilah. So unbecoming...

Unbecoming. That was why Louisa allowed it. If William was raping Del, he wouldn't bother his wife. Sex was an untidy, messy business the lady didn't want to mess with. Never mind that her daughter was being assaulted in the other wing. It kept up for two long months, the entire summer before Del would have started her junior year in high school. Manda had gone to visit her grandmother in Corpus Christi and both Blake and Vance were away at some kind of sports camp for part of the summer and then they had a trip to Ireland that Blake's mother paid for.

Del had been alone. She had plenty of casual friends, but she hadn't trusted any of them enough to tell them what was happening. Her own mother pretended ignorance or accused Del of lying. Who else was she going to turn to?

Del had been so humiliated, so mortified. Completely alone, terrified, ashamed and she hadn't known what to do when William first showed up in her room.

At first, it had been oral sex. The humiliation of that had been bad enough but after a few weeks, he had gotten bored with it. He started raping her, once, twice and sometimes three nights a week. The few times she tried to fight, he beat her until she blacked out from the pain and then he raped her while she was unconscious.

The last time, he'd come in and looked at her, that cruel smile on his mouth. She'd snapped. She picked up her lamp and threw it at him. It caught him on the shoulder and she'd tried to run past him but he had grabbed her and shoved her to the ground, face first. He'd held her down with his knee digging into her back. He tore off the thick flannel pajamas and her underwear but instead of forcing himself in like he usually did, he'd…

Instinctively, Del clenched her buttocks together. If she thought the rapes were bad, they were nothing compared to the pain she'd experienced when he sodomized her. She'd been bleeding when he left and continued to bleed off and on for two days. She'd been a mess of bruises, despair and desperation when she climbed off the floor and went into the shower and she had only one thing in mind.

Getting the hell out.

She'd sworn she wouldn't ever come back, either.

So what was she doing here now? Del heaved out a sigh and pushed away from the sink. She left the bathroom and went over to the bed. It was piled high with fat comforters and warm blankets and fluffy pillows. She grabbed a pillow and clutched it her chest as she leaned back against the headboard.

No matter how much she'd missed her friends, she hadn't wanted to come back here. But she was tired of living in fear and if that meant returning home, even for just a few days, she'd damn well do it.

ಬಿ

"She's doin' *what?*" Blake repeated. He lowered his coffee cup and looked at Joe, searching for some sign the old man was pulling one over on him. All he saw was a puzzled look. Yeah, Blake was a little puzzled himself. "You're serious. Deedee works at a homeless shelter?"

Joe swiped a cloth down the already pristine counter and shrugged. "That's what I heard from Maude. Does counseling type stuff for runaways and that sort of thing. Up in Cincinnati."

His wife Maude had no doubt heard it through the grapevine. "I don't believe it," Blake muttered.

Joe nodded toward the door. "Well, you can ask for yourself. She's on her way in here with her cousin."

Blake's heart leaped inside his chest. He hoped nothing he felt showed on his face as he turned and looked out the big window. He saw Vance. His old football buddy was still as big as he'd been in high school, but some of the hard muscle had softened. His wife didn't seem to mind. She said he was like a big teddy bear now. And every time she said it, Vance blushed like a girl.

The woman at his side, though, didn't look a damn thing like Deedee Prescott. Her hair was dark, nearly black. It was hard to tell with the way she had it braided, but it looked straight as a pin, too. Dee had the most beautiful, amazing blonde curls, curls that looked almost too perfect to be real. A pale blonde that on most people, he'd say came out of a box, but he knew in detail just how natural a blonde she was.

Deedee had dressed like the princess she was, wearing cute, flirty clothes that showcased her pinup girl body.

The woman who walked beside Vance had a weird Goth/punk thing going on. There was a black cord around her neck and Blake caught sight of something silver hanging from it. The shirt she wore was form fitting, outlining a rather magnificent pair of breasts before disappearing into a pair of loose, almost baggy pants that she kept cinched around her waist with a wide belt. Thick-soled boots completed the ensemble.

She looked like she was dressed to fight, Blake realized. Well, maybe not fight. She didn't look like she was out cruising for trouble, but she sure as hell looked ready to deal with it if it happened her way. This dark haired woman carried herself with a tense, wary grace, ready to defend herself or take off running. Like she'd had to do both in the past, and she was prepared to do either or both again.

The bell over the door chimed and Vance held the door open. The woman stepped through and Blake almost turned away. That wasn't Deedee. But then her eyes met his and his heart stopped.

Oh, shit.

Those pretty, misty green eyes were unmistakable. He had dreamed about those eyes more times than he cared to remember. But her gaze wasn't so soft now—hell, with the exception of the breasts straining under the thin cotton of her shirt, nothing about her looked soft.

She wasn't just dressed to fight. She was *prepared* to fight.

He'd been wrong. That was Deedee, all right, but she'd changed. The sweet, fun party girl she had been in high school was gone, long dead if the look in her eyes was any indication. The woman in front of him had nothing sweet or fun inside her.

Something hard and cold settled inside him as he studied her.

The look in her eyes, unfortunately, wasn't one he was unfamiliar with. He knew it all too well. Prescott was a small town in a small county, but it wasn't Mayberry. Bad shit happened here. The average citizen could overlook it, many were probably unaware of it. A man working for the sheriff's office didn't have the luxury of not seeing it, though.

The kind of things that caused the hardness he saw in Deedee's eyes were the kind of things that made him hate his job. That look came from going through hell, kicking and screaming. Not everybody made it through the journey and many who did make it through were broken. All of them were different.

Nobody could survive a trip through hell and not be a different person on the other side. Dee had taken that trip but she hadn't emerged broken. No, she was stronger. Harder.

What in the hell had happened to her?

A sick, ugly rage started to form inside him and for a minute, Blake saw nothing but red. Every protective instinct he had came snarling to the surface and the adrenaline that crashed through him had his heart pounding, his fists clenching.

Breathing through the rage took every shred of control he had.

෨

Vance said something and Del smiled a little. She'd forgotten what a goofball the big guy was. After the first few minutes, she hadn't felt so awkward around him and she was glad. At least she still felt like there was somebody she could call family.

"So you seen Blake yet?" Vance asked, his voice too casual.

"No," Del said, trying to sound as casual as her cousin but she had a feeling she failed.

"Manda talk about him much?"

With a restless shrug, Del said, "Just to say he was still around. We had a lot of catching up to do." Actually, they'd spent the afternoon making the almost careful small talk that two casual acquaintances might have.

After Manda's too insightful questions, Del had backpedaled and Manda, bless her heart, had let her. As graceful as you could please, Manda guided the conversation back in safe territory and safe didn't include much mention of anything other than the weather, the new elementary school and whether or not the town was going to need yet a third doctor in a few years. And, of course, the reunion.

She looked up at Vance and saw that he was looking at the Sheriff's car parked outside of the diner. She smiled faintly. "Don't tell me Blake's run wild." He had always had a streak of it in him, but just a little. Enough to give him a mischievous charm.

"Well...." Vance drawled the word out, long and slow, as he scratched his chin. "He did do that, a bit. But it's been a while. He's actually with the Sheriff's department now, second in command, as a matter of fact."

Del arched a brow. "Really." Blake as a cop. Well, technically, a deputy. But it all added up the same thing. She tried to wrangle him into that image, the memory of the boy she'd loved, but it didn't quite gel.

"Yeah. He...ah...well." Vance stopped in his tracks and waited for Del to look at him before he said anything. He didn't try to touch her. It was weird, too, because she remembered that Vance was very much a touchy-feely kind of guy. He gave big bear hugs, he tugged on hair, he patted shoulders and backs. But all he had done was shake her hand. He'd tried to hug her, she remembered, when they'd run into each other in Cincinnati and she'd backed away.

She should have hugged him and gotten it over with, because Vance, for all his teasing and joking, saw people too clearly. He stood there, looking just a little older, but a lot wiser. His voice was quiet as he said, "Blake was sick for a while, Del. He had cancer."

The pit of her stomach opened up and dropped out. She felt everything solid inside of her dissolve, felt her heart stop and a scream of denial echoed inside her head. And all of it silent. She never said a word and she didn't bat an eyelash. Showing any kind of emotion revealed weakness, as far as Del was concerned, and she didn't allow herself any weaknesses.

So she waited until she was certain she could speak normally before she asked, "Had?"

Vance shrugged. If he was disturbed by her lack of response, he didn't show it. "Hodgkin's Disease. Spent a few years getting all sorts of treatments up in Louisville. The doc declared him cancer free and he's doing good."

"And you're telling me because..."

Vance just smiled and shrugged. "Just so you're warned. Lots of things stayed the same 'round here. But a few things changed...I'm not only talking about you," He cocked his head and smiled at her, a little sadly, she thought.

Del was prepared for anything—okay, just about anything. She thought maybe Blake would look sick and weak. Maybe he was older, heavier, there could be a dozen things and Del told herself she was prepared. But the man standing at the counter talking to Joe wasn't what she'd prepared for.

He was taller than she remembered. Much more so. Broader through the shoulders, although his hips and waist were as lean as she remembered. His long form had filled out and she suspected there was a lot of muscle hiding under the simple, white dress shirt. A plain, black leather belt held his badge and his weapon. He looked completely comfortable with both, and both suited him a lot better than Del would have imagined.

His eyes were the same blue. Robin's egg-blue, she used to tease him because they were an exact match for the Crayola crayons she used to color with when she was a child. Robin's egg had been her favorite. Thick, golden brown hair used to tumble into those eyes. Del had loved playing with that hair, pushing it back from his forehead, teasing him that his hair curled almost as much as hers.

Not anymore.

It didn't look like he had any. His eyebrows weren't blonde anymore either, but a stark black on his tan, lean face. His eyes were still that amazing blue, surrounded by lashes that would make a model envious. The black cloth covering his head didn't look anything like a fashion statement and she had a feeling he cared about as much for fashion now as he had when they'd been younger.

She'd been the clotheshorse. Jeans and a T-shirt had always suited Blake just fine and he'd looked damn nice in them, too. He'd filled them out good in high school, but now...*whoa.*

Yeah, he'd changed all right. His face was harder and

his eyes held a weary cynicism. It hurt some, seeing that. The boy had been a heartstopper—all her teenage fantasies, before she'd stopped having them, had centered around that beautiful face and clever mouth. The reality of the man he'd become was every bit as mesmerizing. Too bad Del had stopped having fantasies a long time ago. He would have taken the starring role.

Despite herself, Blake still had the ability to make her heart race and her mouth go dry. She almost wished she remembered how to have a fantasy. One about Blake would be a welcome respite from the nightmares that usually came visiting while she slept.

When he started in their direction, Del almost turned and darted out the door. She didn't want to see him yet. She decided she might be ready to talk to him, over distance, in a few more years. Ten. Twenty, tops.

But she didn't run.

Del had come here to put running behind her—not run away the first time she came face to face with her ex.

He stopped a few feet in front of her and Del held herself still as he looked her over, starting at the thick-soled boots on her feet and traveling upwards. His eyes lingered on her hair and she braced herself for the questions. They didn't come, though. Instead, he just smirked a little and said, "Nice to see you again, Deedee."

His voice was soft and casual, not showing one hint of the betrayal he'd felt when he had come home and his girl was gone. She hadn't called him, hadn't left him any kind of note—Deedee had just been *gone*. This was the first time Blake had seen her in twelve years, but he wasn't prepared for it.

Not one bit.

Her eyes met his, solemn and unsmiling. Her mouth was naked and set in a flat, unyielding line. Deedee had loved to laugh but the cool stranger standing before him didn't look like she knew how. He held his hand out. She hesitated before placing her hand in his. Her nails were unpainted. Blake didn't think he'd ever seen her look so— bare. No makeup. No jewelry that he could see, except for that black cord around her neck. It had some sort of pendant on it, but it was hidden under the high neck of her shirt. No earrings.

Nothing.

Her voice was soft, huskier than he remembered. "I go by Del now."

Her eyes dropped to his hand and he realized he was still holding hers Instead of letting go, he squeezed gently. Her eyes widened and her pupils flared a little. She tugged on her hand and slowly, he let go. He watched as her hand closed into a fist. In the base of her throat, he could see her pulse slamming away.

The bell hanging over the diner's door jangled and Blake lifted his gaze. The woman standing just behind Deedee's shoulder still looked a lot like Deedee, thanks to plastic surgery. Or rather, she looked a lot like he would have expected Deedee to look.

Well, if Deedee had been the soulless bitch her mother was.

35

"Hello, Blake. Have you seen Delilah?" Louisa's voice dripped with a rich, cultivated southern accent, just a little too high society for Prescott, Tennesee. It was a pretty enough voice, but it had about the same effect on Deedee that Blake would have expected if she had swallowed a live rat.

A look of rampant disgust and distaste crossed her face before she carefully blanked her features. Except her eyes. Her eyes were cold as ice. Blake shifted so he could still see her face as she looked at her mother.

"Louisa."

Louisa's eyes went wide. *"Delilah?"* One ringed, manicured hand fluttered up and she touched her throat. "My word. Is that you?"

"Yes." As she stared at her mother, something moved through her. Del had no idea what she thought she was going to feel, seeing her mom again. But thankfully, there was none of the hurt or betrayal that had pushed her to crying so many times. Just anger—and distaste.

Del had been told often enough growing up that she had a lot of her dad on the inside, and her mother on the outside. Right now, she wished she'd looked more like her dad than her mom. Of course, it was that part of her that came from Dad that gave her the strength to stand in front of her mother right now.

"My. Haven't you grown up? Your hair is absolutely charming." Louisa recovered quickly. She was too hung up on herself not to. Del figured nothing she did or said would have too much of an effect on Louisa. Well, maybe one thing. But she wasn't going to relive her personal hell just to get back at her mother. "I simply can't believe you didn't let me and your father know you were coming to town."

Del curled her lip. "That bastard is not my father." She dropped her voice and took a step closer. She leaned in and put her mouth on level with her mother's ear. "You call him that, ever again, and you will be sorry." Louisa inhaled sharply, and satisfied that her mother had gotten the point, Del stepped back.

Louisa's expression never changed but her eyes glinted like green ice. "I heard that you are staying at Manda's. I know you must have so much to catch up on, but I've missed you. Won't you come stay at home?"

"Oh, yeah. Like I'm going to do that. *Not.*"

Louisa's hand flew out and caught Del's wrist. *What the...* There was a very, very strange look in Louisa's eyes as she dug her nails into Del's wrist. "Darling, you must. There is so much for us to talk about."

Del twisted her hand and shoved, breaking her mother's grip with a single, effective move. She'd had to use it a time or two before. Once she'd gotten some kind of hold back on her life, self defense was the first goal she had set for herself. She wouldn't ever be helpless again. Not ever. After the first few months, she was able to walk down the street with her head help up and she could look other people in the eye again.

Aside from the confidence it gave her, which was something of a miracle in itself, it came in handy in her line of work. The kids she worked with, for the most part, were victims. But after a while, some victims had a bad habit of becoming the victimizer. The regular self-defense courses were one way she had of making sure she didn't become one of the victimized again. *Never again.* It didn't happen too often, but occasionally she did have to use some of the self-defense skills. While she'd been forced to use it a few times, it hadn't ever felt so damned good. Not until now. Del smiled a little. "Mother dear, there is nothing for us to talk about. Not now. Not ever." She gave Louisa a cold, brittle smile. "Leave. Me. Alone."

She glanced at Blake. Sadness filled her. He was watching her with that same, intent stare she remembered from high school. Like she was the only person in the room. And it still had the weird affect of making her heart dance in her chest. If she wasn't so screwed up inside... She cut off the *what if* thoughts before they could fully form.

What ifs were fairy tales and Del was damaged goods. She wasn't so messed up that she couldn't realize it was the victim inside her talking. She did all the things she knew she was supposed to. She had a small, select group of friends she could talk to and there was even a support group she hit when things got too rough. The other stuff, she dealt with, attending her meetings faithfully and she was determined she wouldn't ever slide down the dark road she'd walked for so long.

But she was also realistic enough to know that getting past all her issues was still a long, long time coming. And it may never come.

Everybody in the diner was looking their way. A few had the manners to pretend otherwise, but Del wasn't fooled. Her reunion with Mommy Dearest was going to be fuel for gossip straight through lunch hour, maybe even into dinner, if nothing else exciting happened in town. Del didn't care. She just wanted to get away from the bitch.

She brushed around Louisa and headed for the door without looking or talking to anybody. She'd apologize to Vance later. Right now, all she wanted was to climb in her car and get back to Cincinnati. That wasn't an option, but at least she could—

The bell jangled over the diner as the door opened. Even before Louisa called out, Del knew who it was. She wasn't lucky enough for Louisa to actually listen to her. She didn't turn around, though. Del kept walking, turning the corner on High Street. Her car was at Vance's office, a block down the road. Louisa called out her name again and Del blew out a breath.

"Might as well get it over with." She stopped walking and turned to wait for her mother. Leaning her shoulder against the window, she glanced inside while she waited for Louisa. Louisa never ran. She strolled in her two-inch pumps like she was taking a walk on the beach.

It gave Del a minute to compose herself and she spent it staring through the window. There were a couple of pieces of canvas on the floor, splashed with paint. Seemed another store was going to open. But right now it was closed and Del had the pleasure of facing her mother without an audience.

Oh, joy.

Now that they were out of hearing range, Del didn't bother to lower or hide her voice. "You obviously didn't get the point, Louisa. I don't want to see you. Period. Not for any reason."

Louisa dropped all motherly affectations and gave Del an icy smile. "I do realize that, Delilah. But you're a Prescott. There are certain expectations of you and you will meet them. Keeping that in mind, I'm planning a small get together. You'll attend naturally—"

Without batting a lash, Del replied, "You wanna bet?" Louisa's eyes narrowed. Twelve or thirteen years ago, Del would have reacted a little different. Faked obedience or worse, she might have done whatever it was that her mother wanted.

But she didn't owe her mother any kind of loyalty. As far as Del was concerned, she didn't even owe Louisa respect.

"Delilah—"

Del lifted a hand and shook her head. "Drop it. Now. Otherwise, I'm going to start recounting just why I don't want to see you. Why I will *not* see him. And I won't be quiet about it. Now go away."

The ice in Louisa's voice all but dripped from her words as she said, "You are a Prescott, Delilah. You will maintain your dignity—"

"Dignity." Del didn't bother to lower her voice. "You're right. Dignity is something to prize when you laying on the floor, bleeding—"

"Delilah." Louisa's face went white and she looked around. Assured that they didn't have an audience, Louisa edged closer. Her smile was brittle and her eyes were sharp. "Prescotts do not air our grievances in public."

"Grievances," Del repeated. "You know what, a grievance would be if I yelled at you because you wouldn't let me stay out past curfew on prom night. A grievance would be me wrecking my car and you refusing to get another one. That's a grievance. Being raped is a hell of a lot more than that."

From the corner of her eye, she saw Louisa lift her hand. Del lifted her chin and said, "Go ahead. Do it. But you ought to know, I fight back now."

Slowly, Louisa lowered her hand. But the look in her eyes clearly said that Louisa wanted to slap her daughter. "I'm not coming to the manor, *Mother.* Get that through your head. I'm not coming for tea, I'm not staying there while I'm in town and if you decide to throw some last minute party, you go right ahead. Just don't count on me being there. I will never step foot in that house so long as you and that bastard live there."

"Regardless of your issues with me and you...William," Louisa corrected when she saw the look on Del's face. "We have things we need to discuss. Family business."

"Family business," Del repeated. She smirked a little and then she outright laughed. "There is no family business that I need to know about, Mother Dear. I've gone twelve years without discussing family business and I'd prefer to go the rest of my life without discussing a damn thing with you. Now, I have things to do."

Chapter Three

Oh, yeah. The party girl was definitely gone. Since she'd walked out of the diner early that morning, Blake had tried to convince himself maybe she hadn't changed as much as he'd thought. It wasn't like they'd said more than a few words to each other.

But he'd been wasting his time. The girl he'd known was long gone. Blake couldn't help but miss her laugh, the way her face glowed when she smiled and the mischievous glint that would appear in her eyes.

It was Thursday night and most of the people coming to the reunion were down at the lake for the barbecue. There were two bonfires going and the attendees roamed back and forth between them, laughing, talking. There was an impromptu karaoke contest running and Blake worked hard to tune out the sound of Vance belting out a very bad rendition of *Live Like You Were Dying.*

The firelight flickered and danced over Dee's face as Blake circled around to stand beside her. "He's no Tim McGraw, is he?"

A smile curved up the corners of her mouth and she glanced towards her cousin. "Definitely not."

He offered her one of the longnecks he grabbed a few minutes earlier and she shook her head. "No, thanks."

"Something besides a beer? Manda couldn't have done better if she paid somebody to set up a cash bar." Blake gestured towards the series of folding tables set up by the tree line.

"No. I'm not into drinking." She'd left her hair loose and Blake watched a long fingered, slender palm come up, shoving the dense, dark hair away from her face, tucking it behind her ear. With the dark hair and the pseudo-Goth clothes, he wouldn't have been surprised to see some serious metal in her ears, or elsewhere.

But she didn't have even a pair of earrings on.

The shirt she wore clung like a second skin and it was just a shade or two darker than said skin, giving the illusion that she wore nothing. Blake had the feeling that if she'd realized how damned sexy a picture she made, she would have found something else to wear.

"So what have you been up to the past ten years, Dee?"

She glanced at him. "Twelve," she corrected in a soft voice. Then she shrugged. "Same as everybody else. Getting by."

"The princess of Pike County ought to do more than get by," Blake teased. It wasn't a nickname she'd cared for and he'd purposely used it to see how she'd react. But he didn't get the reaction he was hoping for. Which would have been any kind of reaction. The only response he got was a faint, polite smile. The kind of smile a person would give a stranger. Empty, meaningless and pointless.

He opened his mouth, about ready to try something else to get a reaction out of her. But instead, he reached out, cupped his hand over her elbow and guided her away from the laughter and the music. She didn't resist but Blake couldn't help noticing that she kept a careful distance between them. As soon as he let go of her arm, she backed away a good five feet.

Out of the blue, a memory flashed through Blake's mind. That last night here at the lake before he left for that camp. The last time he saw Dee. They'd come down to the lake with plans to swim, fish and stay gone until way past curfew. When he'd picked Dee up, she had worn a pair of cut offs and a pale blue bikini. By the time night fell, it had cooled off and she'd ended up wearing an old denim shirt of his.

Manda had been down by the shore with Brad, while Blake and Dee were standing in possibly this same spot. Dee had her back against a tree. He could still remember how she looked, moonlight filtering down through the trees, her curls in a wild tumble around her face and shoulders. She'd reached for him, lifted her mouth to his. They'd been just a few seconds away from making love for the first time that night. Dee wouldn't have said no, Blake didn't think. But he was leaving in the morning for two months and he didn't want to their first time to be followed by a separation.

Who ever would have thought a twelve-year old memory would have the power to turn his blood to lava? Hunger raged inside him and when he focused on Dee's face, it was almost like he was staring at her through a time warp. He could see the dark hair, straight as a pin, falling to her shoulders and the plain, almost ugly utilitarian clothes and the unsmiling set of her face. But the memory of that last night kept superimposing itself and he saw her smiling and laughing, her arms reaching for him and her mouth opening for his.

"What happened to you, Dee?"

She lowered her lashes, shielding her gaze from him. "I don't know what you mean."

"Bull." Blake closed the distance between them, watching her the entire time. She didn't move away. But everything about her went on edge. He could see it. Her body tensed. He could see her open her hands, flexing them, before closing them into tight fists.

"Something happened," he murmured. He reached down and captured one wrist, lifting it. She resisted but he didn't let go. He looked from her fisted hand to her face. "You look like you're afraid of me, Dee."

Her voice shook as she said, "I'm not afraid of you, Blake." She tugged on her hand but he didn't let go. Dipping his head, Blake kissed her knuckles. They'd gone white, she had her hand fisted so tight.

Not afraid? Yeah, like he was going to believe that. She was scared and she'd take off running if she could get away from him. He wanted to pull her close and soothe her, chase away whatever it was that had put those shadows in her eyes. Without even thinking about it, Blake started to stroke his thumb back and forth across her wrist.

Dee's eyes widened, her pupils flared and her mouth went tight. She jerked against his hold again and Blake kissed her knuckles again, rubbed his thumb across the delicate skin of her wrist. "Talk to me, Dee."

There were ridges on her soft skin—they didn't register at first. Dee continued to struggle against his hold, harder, almost desperate. She managed to turn her wrist a little, pulling it in closer to her chest.

Alarm, understanding, they managed to filter through all the other thoughts circling through his head. Blake narrowed his eyes. He pulled on her wrist and moved closer. "Let me see your wrist, Dee. Now."

"Let me go," she said. Her voice was shrill, panicky. In the dim moonlight, she looked whiter than death.

"Let me see your wrist," he repeated.

Del twisted violently in his arms and he ended up backing her against the tree. She went crazy. She struggled against him, brought up her knee to rack him, tried to bite him—even managed to sink her teeth into the muscled part of his forearm. He just barely avoided her knee, catching it on his thigh and hissing at the impact.

"Calm down," he ordered.

But it was almost like she couldn't even hear him. Dee's struggles grew even more frenzied. She was strong and she fought like a demon too. A demon who knew how to fight. She slammed her foot down on his instep and he grunted in response. In self-defense, he whirled her around and wrapped her in a bear hug to pin her arms.

At that angle, she couldn't do much more than kick at his shins. Or so he thought. She reared back with her head and caught him in the nose. Pain flared hot and bright but he didn't let go.

He almost did, when she started to cry. Rage burned inside him, a slow fuse at first, but with every soft, muffled sob, it grew hotter and brighter until it felt like a supernova had settled inside his gut. He wanted to tear something apart with his hands. No. Someone. But he couldn't do that until he knew who it was he had to kill.

There was a someone too. He had no doubt about that. This kind of reaction didn't come from nowhere. As soon as Dee said the name, Blake was going to kill him. Screw his badge. Screw his job. He was going to kill the bastard who had put this fear inside his girl.

His girl... Fuck.

How weird that he realized it here, in the dark woods, while she struggled and cried and fought to get away from him. She'd been out of his life for twelve years and during that time, the both of them had gone through different kinds of hell. But Dee was still his.

Slowly, her struggles eased and then she stopped fighting. Her head fell forward and she stood there, sobbing and trying hard not to.

Del was suffocating. Air wheezed in and out of her lungs in harsh, painful gusts and she still felt like something was smothering her. There was a soft, soothing rumble at her ear and dimly, she realized it was Blake, talking to her. His hands no longer restrained her and for a second, she almost broke away.

She wanted to run, run away, as far as she could go, as fast as she could go. But her legs wouldn't move and she couldn't breathe past the sobs that were choking her.

Gently, he turned her around in his arms, so that she was sobbing against his chest and this time, when he tried to look at her wrist, Del didn't have the energy to fight him. His thumb stroked down the scar. It was long and thin with an almost surgical neatness. He lifted the other wrist and studied the matching scar and then he cupped her chin in his hand. "If I ask why, will you tell me?"

Del shook her head, mute.

His eyes went hard. Then his lashes lowered and when he looked back at her, there was nothing of the anger she'd sensed inside him. "You will. Maybe not now. But you will." Then he lifted her hand and pressed his lips to one scarred wrist, then the other.

She gasped at the feel of his lips touching her. Del hadn't willingly let a grown man this close to her in years. More than a decade. It wasn't exactly an innocent touch, his warm mouth pressing against the scars. But it wasn't a sexual touch either, no matter what she had seen in his eyes earlier. *All better...*

If only it was that easy. "Let me go," she whispered, her voice hoarse. Her throat hurt from the crying jag and her head was all muffled. All she wanted was to go home. But home was too far away right now and Del had promised herself she'd stop running.

So Manda's. She wanted to go back to Manda's, climb into her bed, cover her head and go to sleep. But Blake wasn't letting go. Not anytime soon anyway. His hand still grasped her wrist lightly and his eyes stayed level on her face. He stood in the shadows, but the moonlight fell through the trees in a way that she could look into his eyes and there was a look there she recognized.

Determination.

With a half-hearted gesture, she tugged on her wrist. "Blake, I just want to go home."

"Fine. I'll take you. We'll talk there."

Panic sizzled through her veins. "No." Shaking her head, she jerked on her hand again and said, "*No*."

"No choice, sweetheart. You can't get there walking. You came down here with Manda and if she sees you right now, she's going to want to know what's wrong. Plus fifty other people will see you and what to know what's going on. So you're stuck with me." He shifted his grip so he could link their hands. "Come on. I'll call Manda from the car."

Too numb to resist, she followed along meekly as he led her through the wood. Blake didn't speak. He didn't ask anything, he didn't say anything. Once they were on the road, he made a call to Manda to tell her he was dropping Del at the house and after that, he didn't say another word. Del opened the door to climb out before he even had a chance to put the car into neutral. But halfway up the sidewalk, her hopes that she'd make it inside without talking to him did a fast crash and burn.

Behind her, she heard the door open and close. She braced herself and turned around, facing him with a lot more bravado than she felt.

"I'm tired. I want to go to bed."

In a soft voice, he murmured, "You want to hide." He nodded towards her wrists. "You want me to leave, then tell me why. I'll go."

She sneered at him, her lip curling before she could stop it. Under her mortification and her shame, she felt a whisper of anger. Del nourished that ember of anger, fanned it to life. That ember flashed, flashing into a full, vibrant life. Shoving her hair back, she said in a cool voice, "Tell you why? Blake, what makes you think I should have to tell you anything? I haven't seen you in twelve years."

"Because you left," he said softly. "You just disappeared out of my life. I'm not asking you to tell me everything that's happened since you left and I'm not expecting you to cry on my shoulder. I just want to know *why*."

He reached out. Instinct had her flinching away but pride kept her from backing up even though she wanted to. He closed his hand over her wrist and lifted it, turning it up, baring the long, thin scar. His thumb rubbed over it and he glanced at her from under the shield of his lashes. "Tell me why."

The look in his eyes was uncompromising. He wasn't going to leave until she gave him something. She had a trite, pat answer that she used on the rare occasion somebody figured it out and asked. It probably wouldn't work on him, even after all this time, he read her better than most. But she wasn't going to go any deeper than that with him.

"Same reason as anybody else does it, Blake. I was screwed up in the head. For a long time. I'm fine now."

Nope. He wasn't buying it. "Screwed up how?"

"Blake..."

He stepped closer until their shoes were touching. This time she couldn't keep herself from backing away. Blake watched and Del couldn't help but feel like he was cataloging and filing away her every move.

"Don't. Don't try to hand me some trite line and don't lie to me." He rubbed his thumb over the thin scar as he slanted a look at her. "If you don't want to explain these, then tell me why you're so afraid of me."

Del stiffened and tried to jerk away from him. "I'm not afraid of you."

"The hell you aren't. You're afraid of me and any other guy that got within five feet of you."

He knew. *Shit.* She could tell by the look in his eyes he had recognized the fear inside of her, and worse, he knew what had caused it. Hell. She shouldn't be surprised. Del had seen her own hell reflected in the eyes of some of the kids she cared for. She could hide it from people who didn't know what to look for but somebody in law enforcement, even in a rinky-dink town like Prescott was going to recognize it.

"It doesn't concern you, Blake," she said. He opened

his mouth to argue and Del lifted a hand. "Please. Don't. I'm holding together by a thread here. I can't handle this right now."

He lifted his hand and this time when he touched her, she managed, just barely, not to flinch. Blake's thumb rubbed over her lips and he whispered, "Twelve years, Dee, and I can't even go a week without dreaming about you. Thinking about you. You didn't even tell me good-bye. You disappeared from my life and I never even knew why. Now you're back here, looking at me with sad, scared eyes and you don't think it concerns me?"

"Blake..."

He placed a finger on her lips and shook his head. "I don't want to hear it, Del. I don't want excuses, I don't want brush offs." He dipped his head and pressed his lips to hers, quick and light. Then he moved away before Del's mind had even processed that he had kissed her.

Del hadn't been kissed in twelve years. Not since that last night at the lake with him. She hadn't wanted to be kissed. But now, even with all the fear and memories crowding her mind, she wished he hadn't moved away quite so fast.

"This isn't over with, Dee. Don't go thinking it is. Go on inside now before I decide I don't want to be so understanding."

He walked away without another word and Del stood there, watching as he climbed into the car. The engine revved to life but he didn't pull out. Finally, she realized he was waiting for her go in. She turned away and ran up the stairs. She fumbled for the key Manda had given her and unlocked the door.

As she locked it behind her, she heard him drive off and she heaved out a sigh. But she wasn't quite certain if the emotion swamping her was relief.

Or regret.

Chapter Four

It was a first for her.

Whether it was just seeing Blake again, or whether it was some fluke, Del really didn't know.

But it was a first...she dreamt of him.

Not the ugly, horrifying dreams that so often woke her out of a dead sleep. But a sweet, hot dream that she really had no desire to interrupt. And it had to be a dream, because in real life, there was no way she could stand so close to him, his hands on her face, his mouth moving against hers, and his body aligned to hers.

His hands slid down her shoulders, his palms brushing the tops of her breasts but she didn't feel any repulsion, nothing but a white-hot streak of heat that raced through her core and set every last nerve tingling.

"You're so pretty," he whispered, lifting his head and staring down at her, a naked adoration on his face. If Blake looked at her like that in real life ever again, she just might cry. But here, in the dream, she could smile teasingly up at him and it felt natural.

Felt right.

Felt perfect.

Taking his hands in hers, she guided them down to her hips and then she slid her arms around his neck and tugged his mouth down to hers. Groaning against his lips, she moved closer—felt the thick ridge of his cock against her belly—

Bare skin to bare skin—

Tearing her mouth away, she stared at him, and then looked down at herself. Her very naked self. "Oh, yeah, this has got to be a dream," she muttered hoarsely.

His eyes met hers and he lifted a hand, cupped her cheek. "Does it matter?"

Del tried to reach for the answer to that. Did it matter that she was having one seriously nice dream about Blake? Or would she rather be awake and doing this?

But there was no sense to be made. Because she realized they weren't alone. There was a pounding, a shrill scream...

Crossing her arms over chest, she hissed and turned her head—and that was all it took. The dream shattered around her and she jerked awake in the bed, sitting upright and staring at the pale blue walls of Manda's guestroom.

Out in the hall, she could hear the baby crying and a horrendous clanging noise. The baby's crying abruptly stopped, the clanging ceased and faintly, Del heard Manda murmuring to the baby.

Itchy, aching and hot, she threw the covers off and rolled up to sit on the edge of the bed. She was *throbbing*—all fricking over. Her breasts ached, her nipples were pulsating and between her thighs, she was almost embarrassingly wet. Deep inside, she felt empty, almost painfully so.

"Geez, Del." Bracing her elbows on her knees, she buried her face in her hands and fought to level out her breathing. "Twelve years without any kind of wet dreams. You sure as hell know how to break a dry spell."

ⅎ

After a long shower and a good thirty minutes spent trying to settle the nerves in her belly, Del left the safety of her room. It had only taken Manda four tries to get her to come out and eat some breakfast. Although Del was so tangled up inside, she doubted she could manage to eat much of anything.

Sitting across the table from Manda, she pushed the bacon and eggs around on her plate and tried to force a few bites down. But after two or three tries, she gave up on the bacon and eggs, settling for a bagel. That much, she might be able to manage.

"There was a message for you last night on the machine when I got home."

Del glanced at Manda over the bagel and frowned. "For me?"

Manda glanced up from the baby she was nursing and nodded. A little wisp of envy curled through Del as she watched Manda with her baby. The little girl had a head of thick, dark curls and big brown eyes. From where she was sitting, Del could see that those big brown eyes were closed right now and the baby's hand stroked Manda's breast as she nursed. Occasionally, she made little humming sounds in her throat that made Del smile.

"It was Beaumont Junior. You remember him?"

Curious now, Del leaned back in the chair. "I think so." Junior was a lawyer, practicing with his father. "Is Beaumont Senior still practicing?"

"Yep. In Hawaii right now with his wife, but he's still going strong. Plays golf once a week, takes his grandkids fishing down on the lake. I hope I'm still living life like he does when I hit my eightieth birthday. Junior's flying solo until his dad gets back but he seemed pretty anxious to talk to you."

"What did he want?"

Manda shrugged. "Beats me. He just said he needed to speak with you and he wants you to call or come by the office while you're in town." She went back to gazing at the baby. There was a look in Manda's eyes, a stunned, wondering kind of awe.

"She's beautiful," Del murmured when the baby finally pulled away from her mother. Manda shifted her up and started to pat her back. It took less than three pats before the baby burped. Del widened her eyes and laughed. "She'd put a lot of men to shame with that one."

Manda laughed. "That's what I thought. You want to hold her?"

No. Absolutely no. But Del couldn't think of a graceful

way to refuse as Manda rose and deposited the baby in her arms. Manda used the blanket thrown over her shoulder to wipe the baby's mouth and then she moved over to the fridge.

While Manda got herself something to drink, Del stared at the baby. An ache settled inside her. This was perfection. Del wasn't unaccustomed to babies. The shelter where she worked as assistant director, sometimes girls came in with babies this young. Too often, Del had been forced to call social services, even as much as hated it. But babies didn't belong in a homeless shelter and those girls, if they were willing, could get help for themselves and their children. Keeping babies in the shelter was a quick way to see the shelter got shut down.

So she wasn't unused to dealing with infants. But this wasn't the same. This wasn't some neglected angel who needed Del's help, but a pampered little doll who cooed and laughed. The baby reached a hand towards Del's face and she smiled. "Hi, Avery." Big eyes widened and the baby squealed. Unable to resist, Del brought the baby closer and nuzzled her round little tummy. The baby giggled and then grabbed at Del's hair. She got hold of one of Del's braids and promptly lifted it to her mouth. "You just finished your breakfast. You don't need a snack," Del said, tugging her hair free. Spying the pacifier on the table, she grabbed it and popped it into Avery's mouth.

Avery started to sniffle and for a second, it looked like she was going to cry. Then her gaze focused on the necklace Del wore. She wrapped her hand around the sturdy leather cord and started to pull. A chair scraped across the floor and Del looked up as Manda sat down with a glass of juice and a bowl of cereal. "Did you write Junior's number down?"

Manda nodded towards the notepad laying on the table. "Yeah." She gave Del an innocent smile. "So what did you and Blake talk about last night?"

"Not much." Del shrugged her shoulders and focused on the baby so she wouldn't have to look Manda in the eye.

"Hmmm. Going to talk about not much with him again?"

Del slid Manda a sidelong glance. "I'm leaving Monday. I live four hours away. There's really no reason to talk about much of anything, is there?"

Manda was quiet as she sipped her juice. She looked down at her breakfast but didn't eat anything. "I don't think he ever got over you. Leaving the way you did, never calling, never writing. I don't think he understood." She looked up and Del saw the hurt in her friend's eyes. "Neither did I."

Silence fell and Del tried to figure out what to say. Finally, she decided she needed to be as honest as she could, without laying herself bare. "I left because I had to. I didn't have any choice. I was messed up for a while. A long while. Took some time to get my head on straight and once I did, I just wanted to move on."

Manda lifted her spoon but instead of eating, she tilted it to the side and watched the milk and cereal splash back into the bowl. "I don't get it, Del. You look like you've seen some rough shit. But when I left, you seemed fine. What changed so fast?"

She knew her voice was harsh but she couldn't control it. "Manda, I can't. Try to understand, I just can't." She shifted the baby to her shoulder and started to rock Avery back and forth. It was an unconscious motion, more to comfort herself than anything else.

Manda was quiet for a long moment and then she sighed. "Okay. But when you're ready, I'll listen."

*Ready...*an hour later, Del left the house. There was no way she'd be ready to look at her high school friend and say *I ran away because it wouldn't stop until I did.*

Climbing into her car, she jammed the key into the ignition but then instead of starting the car, she just sat there. One hand rested on the wheel, the other on the key. "I'm so tired of this," she muttered. Her voice was thick with tears and for once, all Del wanted was to let those tears fall. She wanted to cry and she didn't want to do it alone.

No, she wasn't ready to tell people about it, but she was tired of letting it rule her life. Even the past few years when she thought she'd finally taken control, those two months twelve years ago colored everything she did, every major choice she made.

She'd spent months running when she had first left. When she left, she took as much jewelry as she could get her hands on and every last bit of cash that was in the house. It had been several thousand dollars worth. If she'd been careful, she would have done okay until she found a place to crash, a place that wouldn't look too closely at her ID. Instead she'd used it to buy drugs, anything, everything that would make her forget. Alcohol and narcotics, she chased the pills with booze, uncaring that it could have killed her.

But none of the pills, none of the liquor could wipe away the memories. They were still there, chasing her into sleep, waiting for her when she woke, haunting her every moment. It was fifteen months after she left when she first started thinking about killing herself.

Her first attempt was a couple months after that, but she'd panicked. After downing a veritable pharmacy, she called 911 and ended up in the ER where they pumped her stomach and called social services. The doctors and nurses there hadn't bought her claims that she was over eighteen. She ended up in the system while they tried to find her parents, but Del wouldn't tell them her real name and surprise, surprise, Mommy Dearest hadn't ever reported her missing.

Social services didn't treat her all that bad. She ended up in a decent foster home with a nice lady with kind, tired eyes. Too kind. Moira Jensen knew what had happened to Del. Not specifically, but she'd recognized the signs, probably the same signs that Blake had recognized. She tried reaching out to Del, and failed. Del hadn't wanted anybody reaching out to her. All she'd wanted was to age out of the system and get away. Very far away.

She might have spent her remaining time, all of five months, with Moira Jensen if a couple of high school jocks hadn't singled her out for their Friday night jollies.

They hadn't raped her, but it had been a close call. Del hadn't gone to the party for any reason other than to score some coke or get drunk.

What she'd gotten was rohypnol and would have been raped if the police hadn't shown up to investigate some calls about a wild party and underage drinking. Although she didn't remember much more than drinking rum and coke, the blackness that followed was almost as terrifying as the memories of what her step-father had done to her.

The shock of it had pushed her too close to those ugly, hated memories and she had run away again, ending up on the streets and the path that would eventually end nearly two years later at a rest stop on Interstate 75 in Ohio, where yet another kind woman would make another rescue attempt. Megan Thomas found Del in a pool of blood. After stopping the bleeding, she'd called 911 and the retired nurse had stayed by Del's side until a social worker showed up to take her place at the emergency room.

That social worker was the one who would eventually pull Del out of hell. Joely Simmons saw the path that Del was following and the stubborn woman refused to let her go any farther. It was because of Joely, even more than Megan, that Del was alive. Alive, clean and sober.

She was the reason that Del had chosen to work with troubled kids—she wanted to help them the way Joely had helped her. Beyond that, Joely was the only person on the planet that knew about every dark, ugly thing in Del's past. When cancer had taken Joely last year, Del had felt as though she'd been cut adrift. Oddly enough, though, when things got rough, she could hear that worn, friendly voice murmuring to her.

Just like now.

You're tired of running, Del, because you've been running for twelve years. Until you face him, face her, face what they did to you and make them deal with you, you'll keep on running.

"I have faced it."

Then why are you still hiding it? Why are you pulling away from people who reach out? People who just want to help?

Her hands shook as she climbed out of the car and her legs wobbled as she headed back up the sidewalk. When she walked into the house, her gut was pitching so hard, she thought she was going to be sick. Those few bites of bagel sat in her belly like a stone. But instead of bolting for the bathroom like she wanted, she went into the kitchen and found Manda at the sink, washing dishes. Manda glanced up. "Forget where the town square was, sweetie?"

"William Sanders raped me."

Glass shattered. The mug that Manda had been washing slipped out of her hands, bounced off the edge of the counter and hit the tile floor. Neither of them noticed. Manda turned towards Del, her eyes wide. "*What?*"

Instinct had Del wanting to backpedal, hard and fast. And she heard that voice, the ghostly voice of a dead friend murmuring to her. *Too late to back off now.* Del swallowed and looked at Manda again. "He raped me. It

64

started two days after y'all left and he kept on doing it until that last night when I ran away."

Manda started for her and Del lifted a hand, shook her head. She couldn't take being touched right now. "Don't. I need to finish this." Her breath squeezed in and out of her lungs like some giant had wrapped a fist around her midsection. "You were gone. Blake was gone. I tried to tell Mama and she laughed, said I was lying. A dirty, nasty lie because I was bored and needed attention and nobody would believe otherwise."

She blinked and saw Manda staring at her with a look of sheer horror on her face. Humiliated, Del turned away and covered her face. That was when she realized she was crying. She scrubbed the tears away.

When Manda touched her arm, Del froze. "My God, Dee. Why... How... *Shit*." Manda moved closer and then she wrapped her arms on Del's waist. Del wanted to pull away but she couldn't. She felt so damn tense, so strung tight, moving might make her shatter into ten thousand pieces.

Slow, shallow breaths—that was the ticket. Del concentrated on each breath, thought about the process breathing in, breathing out, and gradually, the clammy fist wrapped around her chest eased up. The nausea eased and she awkwardly patted Manda's back. "Give me a minute." When Manda's arms loosened, Del slipped away. Her legs wobbled beneath her as she made her way to the counter. There was a mug drying in the dish rack. Sticking it under the faucet, she filled it and drank the tepid water. Her throat was still dry but her belly pitched and roiled as the water hit.

I'm not going to get sick. I'm not going to get sick. I'm not—

"Sit down." Manda's hand closed over Del's arm and the smaller woman more or less manhandled Del into a chair. Then she pressed her palm to the back of Del's neck and forced her over until she was staring at the floor. "Stay there."

The water was running again. It seemed far too loud. Little black dots danced in her vision. "You're hyperventilating," Manda said from close behind her. Del flinched as something cold and wet touched her neck. "Take some deeper breaths, sweetie. Slow it down."

In a reedy voice, Del said, "I'm good. Let me up." She sat up and stared into Manda's eyes. Tears swam in her brown eyes and she looked like she was caught between hurt, fury and pity. Pity—that was the last thing she wanted.

"I don't know if I want to wring your neck for not telling me or go and kill him." Manda's voice shook with fury and her hands kept opening and closing into fists.

"It's not the easiest thing to talk about," Del said. Her hands were shaky, she realized absently. She stared at them. Her cuticles were cracked and her nails short. There had been a time when her hands could have done a Palmolive commercial, perfectly manicured, soft and smooth, her nails done some fru-fru shade of pink.

Del hadn't had a manicure in so long she couldn't remember how it felt. The ends of her hair caught her gaze and she reached up, caught one braid in her hand. The dark brown wasn't ugly. It wasn't pretty, either. It was just—ordinary. The entire point. She went out of her way to blend in, to look as plain as she could. For a long time, she'd worn clothes so baggy she could hide in them, but then she started the self-defense classes and somebody pointed out how easy it was to grab onto baggy clothes and turn them into a weapon to use against her.

Everything she did, everything she said, every choice she made, all of them were shaped by something that had happened twelve years ago. She hadn't gone out on dates, she avoided relationships because she didn't want to risk anybody getting close enough to see below the surface.

William Sanders had taken away her innocence and her youth—but she might as well give him the rest of her life if she kept going on like this. "I'm letting him win," she said in a flat, emotionless voice. "God."

Del blew out a harsh, frustrated breath and looked back up at Manda. "I know the behavior. I see it in others and I can recognize it. Why didn't I see it this clearly in myself?"

Manda shook her head. "It doesn't matter because you see it now." She reached out and clasped Del's hands in hers, rubbing them. "You going to fix it?"

℘

Fix it. It sounds so easy. Del drove down the highway, operating on autopilot as she drove towards town.

How did she fix it? Almost made it sound like her carburetor had gone out. At least that she could take to a mechanic. Fixing herself was a lot more complicated. She was coping okay, Del supposed but she was a very long way from *being* okay and it made all the difference in the world. She was operating in a vacuum and all of a sudden, she was tired of just existing. Maybe it had been seeing Manda with the baby. Maybe it had to do with seeing her mother again for the first time in a decade and finally acknowledging what lay under that pretty, polished exterior. Or maybe it had to do with seeing Blake again.

Blake...

Her heart did a weird little dance in her chest as she thought about him. She hadn't thought seeing him would hit her like this. Make her legs go all weak and wobbly and her belly twist with a queer ache—an emptiness. She remembered the sensations. That crooked grin of his had turned her insides to mush from the time she'd been old enough to notice and time had only added to his appeal.

She pulled into one of the parking spaces in front of the Sheriff's office and shut off the engine. But instead of climbing out, she just sat there, reminding herself to breathe and gripping the steering wheel so tight it wouldn't have surprised her if the vinyl cracked. Her belly pitched and she closed her eyes. She didn't want to do this.

Telling Manda had been hard. Almost impossible. Telling Blake—even thinking about it made her feel like her skin had shrunk, leaving her feeling tight and itchy. All the while, shame did a slow, insidious spin inside her.

Her heart beat with a force that made it hard to breathe and before she even realized it, she reached out to start the car. *Can't do this can't do this can't—*

The car made a weird sputtering sound as the engine tried to turn over and oddly enough, that was enough to jar her out of the panicked mindset. "He's controlled enough of your life," Del whispered. Before she could change her mind, she jerked the keys out of the ignition and climbed out of the car. The sun shone down bright and hot on her shoulders but she was cold. Crossing her arms over her middle, she headed into the Sheriff's office.

Thanks to her job, Del wasn't a stranger to police departments. Too often, she'd have to take one of her kids to the cops to get them to file restraining orders—and on the rare occasion, she'd been forced to turn a few of them in. The rules of the shelter were strict and neither Del or the director would allow them to be broken. Anybody caught selling or buying drugs while in the shelter was turned in.

She'd certainly spent enough time in these sort of places. The small rural office of the Pike County Sheriff wasn't that much different. It was quieter than she was used to, but she could still hear the murmur of voices. A raised voice—somebody pissed off because he'd violated a restraining order, and the softer tones of some deputy trying to calm the offender down.

A woman Del didn't recognize sat at the desk up front and she looked up at Del with a polite, quizzical smile. Her voice shook as she asked, "Is Blake Mitchell available?"

The words had just left her mouth when she felt him standing behind her. Slowly, she turned and looked at him, unaware of how pale she looked. He stood in the doorway of a small office. It looked about the size of her work cubicle but it had a door—that meant the door could be closed and she could have a little bit of privacy while she broke down.

That was good. Because she *was* going to break. Very, very shortly.

Blake's blue eyes darkened with concern as he studied her and the gentleness in his voice made her want to weep. "What's the matter, Dee?"

"We need to talk." Her voice came out as a faint whisper, but it was a wonder she could speak at all, considering how damn tight her throat had gotten.

Blake simply stood aside and she shuffled past him into the office. Okay, maybe it was *too* small, she thought. The walls seemed to close in on her as he closed the door. He edged around her, taking care not to touch her as he moved behind the desk and bent down. When he straightened up, he held a Coke in his hand. It fizzed as he popped it open and held it out to her. She wasn't thirsty but since it gave her a reason to stall, she accepted it. "Can't keep anything to drink in the break room," he said, his voice casual. "People keep stealing them so I bought one of those mini fridges that you can lock."

Del lifted the can took her lips and took a tiny sip. *God, how do I do this?* she thought desperately. She didn't *want* to do this. Not at all.

She looked about as fragile as a piece of spun glass, Blake thought. He wanted to go to her and hold her, but like glass, he had a feeling she would shatter too easy right now. Her hands held the red aluminum can like it was a lifeline and they were shaking so that some of the soft drink had spilled but she didn't even notice.

"Dee." No response. "Del...Del, look at me."

She blinked and looked up at him. Hell, her eyes were glassy and her lips were pale, all but bloodless. As she stared at him, she swayed just a little and Blake swore in silence as he moved close enough to catch her if she started to fall. She didn't though. She looked down at the can in her hands and then set it down on the desk. Then she wiped her hands on her pants before closing them into tight fists. She said something and it was so soft, so faint, he wasn't sure he heard her right.

Fury lit inside him and he throttled it down as he edged closer. She had her chin tucked against her chest and he could tell her eyes were shut. "Look at me, Dee," he said quietly.

Slender shoulders rose and fell as she took a deep breath. Then she looked up at him. Tears shone diamond-bright in her eyes but she blinked them away before they could fall.

"What did you say?"

"It was my stepfather."

The fury went from a smoldering fuse to a nuclear meltdown and it took everything inside him not to leave the office, then and there, drive to out to the Prescott manor and kill William Sanders, slow and painful. His voice was raspy as he asked, "When?"

"That summer."

Blake's hands closed into fists. "I'm going to kill him." Slow. He was going to kill him, nice and slow, and he was going to enjoy every damned second of it. That was the only thought in his head, but then he looked at her. Saw the tears she was trying to hold back, saw the way she stood there, shaking.

She spun away from him and he watched as she lifted her hands and covered her face. Her spine bowed forward, like the burden she was carrying inside had just become too much. The murderous rage didn't fade, but in that moment, he couldn't leave her any more than he could cut off his own arm.

Slowly, Blake took a deep breath and tore his mind away from the ways he wanted to maim, dismember and hurt William Sanders. That could wait. Not for long, but it could wait. Dee, on the other hand, couldn't.

"That's why you left."

She gave a slight nod. Blake blew out a ragged breath and reached up, rubbing the back of his neck. Okay. He could handle this. He had known something bad happened to her, knew she had most likely been raped—it was in the way she carried herself, the changes in her. He just hadn't expected it to be somebody he knew. "Can you tell me?"

A harsh sob left her and Blake reached for her. He just couldn't stop it. She flinched but didn't pull away.

Keeping his touch gentle and light, he rested his hands on her waist, doing his damnedest not to make her feel trapped, prepared for the fact she was going to pull away from him. But instead, she leaned into him. Just a little. Just slightly. Her voice was halting at first, and then she started to talk faster and faster, until she was all but tripping over the words as they poured out of her.

All the while, horror and rage mingled inside of him, forming an ugly, volatile cocktail that was just waiting to implode. It had started right after he left, and kept up almost the entire damned summer. She'd lived in two months of hell and he hadn't known. He hadn't been able to help her. *Two fucking months—*

But that wasn't the worse part, he realized as Del explained she'd told her mother. He hadn't thought he could get more pissed—obviously, he'd been wrong. Now his fury how had two targets. "You told your mother," he repeated, his voice flat.

Del nodded, opening her mouth to say something but nothing came out. "You've already come this far, Del. Get it all out," he murmured, but she shook her head. Gently, he cupped her face and forced her to look at him.

Her green eyes were glowing with fury and pain, her mouth twisted as she snarled, "She told me to stop telling such *unbecoming lies.*"

Then the dam broke. She started to cry, her entire body shuddering with the force of the sobs racking her and Blake stood there, helpless. She burrowed against him and he wrapped his arms around her as he silently damned Louisa and William Sanders into the lowest level of hell.

It went beyond his understanding, a mother accusing her daughter of something like that. The hideous thing though, he could picture Louisa doing just that. *Unbecoming lies.* Blake wanted to strangle them. The both of them, Louisa for being so cold and callous. Sanders for being a perverted monster. His gut knotted with shame as he realized that he had been living in a town with people capable of such cruelty and he'd never realized it. He hadn't ever cared for Louisa or William Sanders but he hadn't thought either of them were much more than self-righteous, self important idiots.

Sanders was a child-rapist. But he wasn't sure what was worse—the child rapist or the woman who had allowed it to happen and never did anything to stop it. The woman who accused her own daughter of lying about something so horrifying.

Del's body shuddered in his arms and he smoothed a hand down her back and murmured to her. He didn't even know what he said. All he knew was that he wanted her tears to stop, wanted to do something to ease the pain inside her.

She burrowed in closer and Blake finally lifted her in his arms and settled down on the floor, his back to the door, legs sprawled in front of him. Del lay awkwardly in his lap and he shifted her around just a little, sliding his arm under her knees and cradling her against him. She continued to cry, crying until her tears soaked his shirt and his arms went numb and still he held her.

When the tears finally stopped, Del tipped her head back to stare at him, her eyes gleaming and her lashes spiky from the tears. Her lids were swollen, her face splotchy from the tears and she was still the most beautiful woman he knew. She always had been—Blake knew in that moment, she always would be. Even when she was ninety-years old and needed a damned cane to walk around, one look at her would hit him like a punch in the gut, hard, fast and breath-stealing.

Her lashes lowered over her eyes and her cheeks turned pink with a blush. She pushed against him. He figured letting her go was about as easy as it would be to cut his arm off, but he did it. Even though doing so made him ache inside.

Del knew that when her head cleared enough, she was going to be humiliated that she had broken down like that. In front of Blake, of all people. Right now, she was too tired. Her throat was raw from the crying jag and she reached for the Coke Blake had given her when they had first come in. It was barely cool when she took a drink. How long had she been crying?

She hadn't ever cried like that. She flicked a glance over at Blake and murmured, "Sorry."

His brows dropped low over his eyes. He was irritated—it was obvious even before he said anything. "Sorry for what?"

Restless, she shrugged. "Breaking down like that. I—"

His hands came down on her shoulders. "Look at me." Reluctantly, she lifted her eyes and met his gaze. "You're entitled to a few tears, Del. Don't apologize for it." His hands tightened and he looked like he wanted to say something else but then he let go of her hands and just stepped away. "So this is why you left? Did your mom send you away to keep you quiet or what?"

The mention of her mother was enough to clear the fog in her brain. With a snort, Del said, "No, although I bet she would have tried that if I had stayed." She squared her shoulders and braced herself to finish it. She hadn't even touched on the worst of it. "I ran away, Blake. I took whatever I could get my hands from the manor, whatever I could sell, and I ran. The money didn't last too long and I ended up living wherever I could. Social services picked me up and I was in the system for a few months. I ran away from the lady they put me with, I got hooked on drugs, I lied, cheated, stole, whatever I had to get by. I never graduated from high school. I was twenty before I got my GED and I did that from a rehab facility."

Unable to look at him any more, she looked down at her wrists and slowly tugged up one sleeve. She traced her index finger down the thin, raised surface of one of the scars. "I'd tried to kill myself a couple of times and always chickened out. This time, I almost succeeded but somebody found me. I ended up in the hospital."

From under her lashes, she saw him reach for her and she held herself still. Long tanned fingers wrapped around her wrist and she found herself staring, mesmerized, as he lifted it up and pressed his lips to the scars. "You look like you expect me to be disgusted," he murmured. He reached for her other wrist and kissed the scars there as well.

He let go of her but he didn't move away. Instead, he moved closer and Del froze as he lifted a hand to cup her face. His lips touched hers, slow and gentle. Del's breath lodged in her throat but he didn't do anything more than that light, soft touch.

Del blinked, a little dazed as he lifted his head to stare at her. "Why did you tell me?"

She swallowed past the knot in her throat. She didn't know how to explain that. Her voice was rusty and hoarse as she answered, "I don't know."

Slowly, she pulled away. She headed for the door, opened it. Then she paused. Without looking at him, she said, "Maybe I didn't want you to keep thinking I ran away from you. I never meant to hurt you, Blake. I never meant to hurt anybody."

She would have left then, but Blake moved to the door. He laid a hand over it, pressing just enough to keep her from slipping out. He combed his fingers through her hair, brushed it away from her neck. His mouth grazed her ear, his voice a soft whisper. "I never got over you, Del. All these years, I thought maybe I could. I knew that I should. But I never did."

Chapter Five

I never got over you.

Del wished he hadn't said that. If she wasn't already messed up enough. It was damned unsettling to realize that she hadn't ever dealt with things. The past four or five years, she thought she'd come to grips with it. Thought she'd dealt with what William Sanders had done, and the insults her mother piled on top of that particular injury.

She hadn't, though.

She slowed down by Beaumont & Beaumont and almost pulled into one of the street-side parking slots. But then she saw the sleek, black Beemer in front of it and pressed on the gas. She hadn't seen her mother but Louisa never drove anything other than a black BMW and Del wasn't about to deal with that particular can of worms on top of everything else.

So instead of going to see what Beaumont Junior wanted, Del pointed her car in the direction of the lake. She'd drive down there and sit by the lake. It used to work. Maybe it still would. As she turned off Main Street onto the two lane highway that led out of town, she dug her phone out of the purse and dialed the lawyer's phone number from memory. It went to straight to voice mail. The recorded voice sounded vaguely familiar and Del tried to place it without success. Man—voice mail in Prescott. Times really had changed around here. It was around lunch time but ten years ago, either the phone went to a plain old answering machine or it wasn't answered. No voice mail.

She left a message with her cell number. Del was starting to think she might hang around a few more days, see if she could put some of her demons to rest before heading back to Cincinnati. God knew she had plenty of personal time coming her way. With that thought in mind, after she disconnected from the voice mail, she called her boss before she could talk herself out of it.

ω

"Damn."

Over the pounding of her heart and the rattle of the chain, Del hadn't heard the door open. She spun around, hands lifted in defense. When she saw Blake standing there, she lowered them. She sucked in air and jerked the gloves off and tossed them on the floor.

The heavy bag was still swinging back and forth and automatically, she reached out and laid a hand on it. "Hello, Blake."

He sauntered into the garage and circled around her.

"You picked up some moves, didn't you, Deedee? You pounding on anybody in particular or just working up a sweat?"

"Del," she corrected automatically. He moved closer and it seemed as though the big garage seemed to shrink, closing in around her. Her face heated as she remembered how she had broken down in front of him. She hadn't thought about it at the time, but later, down at the lake, Del realized the entire time she'd been crying, he had been holding her and she hadn't once felt afraid.

Blake moved closer and despite herself, Del felt that familiar panic rear its ugly head and she battled it back down. Blake wouldn't hurt her. She knew that, knew it enough so that she really didn't feel that threatened even when he closed in on her personal space, eliminating more distance between them.

He brushed a damp strand of hair back from her face, his fingers lingering on the curve of her neck. "How are you?"

"Fine." Inanely, she asked, "You?"

A faint grin came and went on his face and he drawled, "Oh, I'm right as rain, ma'am." His lids drooped, shielding his gaze, but there was no mistaking the lazy, lambent look in his eyes. She felt frozen in place as he looked down at her. He seemed to take in every single thing about her, seeing beyond the too-loose pants, the form-fitting shirt and drab brown braids. Those eyes of his had always seen too deep. He saw so much of her and Del hated it. Hated how he made her feel. These yearning, needy feelings were just a disaster waiting to happen. She'd gone twelve years not letting anybody get too close, physically and emotionally. Even if she had finally admitted to herself that she was far from okay, she didn't know if she was ready to risk letting somebody get close again.

Especially not Blake. He had an advantage over most, considering he'd been her first, and only, love. She'd always figured she'd romanticized her memories of him but looking at him, she had to wonder.

He was still so ridiculously good looking, more so now than he had been in high school. Those fine, chiseled features of his belonged in Hollywood, not in Prescott, Tennessee, a small town in the middle of nowhere. Impossibly blue eyes and a mouth she could still remember feeling against hers. She had the odd urge to reach up and pull off the black cloth covering his head. Plain and simple, she wanted to reach out and touch him.

Del hadn't wanted to touch anybody in so damn long. And it scared the hell out of her.

Maybe it's time you did...

That voice seemed to come from all those wishful, wistful yearnings. Common sense told her something else. Carefully, Del edged around him, circling away without really appearing to run. "Do you need something, Blake?"

He shrugged, still moving forward with that slow, lazy grace. Gently, he asked, "Are you afraid of me, Del?"

Disgusted with herself, she planted her feet and met his gaze levelly. "Of you? Not exactly." She shrugged her shoulders and admitted, "Of men in general? Yeah."

He nodded and murmured, "I get that. What if I want to touch you? Should I ask? Should I not bother? If I told you that I wanted to kiss you, would you tell me to get back in my car and just leave you the hell alone?"

Fear had her shaking. Her voice was almost non-existent and she couldn't decide who was more surprised when she said, "No."

Blake's eyes darkened and he closed the distance between them and dipped his head. He pressed his mouth to hers, keeping the touch light and gentle. He gave her plenty of room to pull away and she was the one who deepened the kiss. She rose on her toes and pressed her mouth against his with a little more pressure.

Del sighed against his lips and that soft, hungry, female sound was sheer torture. At the same time, it was sheer bliss. Blake wanted nothing more than to grab her and hold her tight against him, taking the kiss deeper, harder. He was greedy for the taste of her and would have done almost anything just to get it, but he didn't do anything. He just stood there and let her kiss him. She licked his lower lip and he felt the blood drain out of his head and straight down to his dick.

It was heaven.

It was hell.

Her hands came up to his shoulders and fisted in his shirt and still Blake wouldn't let himself touch her. His restraint was rewarded when she stroked her tongue along his lips and when he opened his mouth, she took the slow, shy caress a little bit deeper. And finally—*finally* he could taste her. Sunshine, sweetness and heat, it was like a drug, even that small taste and all he wanted was *more*.

Instead, he lifted his head and made himself ease back. Del's eyes were closed but when he retreated, her lashes lifted and he found himself staring into foggy, almost dazed green eyes. She swayed closer and this time when she touched him, he reached up and covered her hand with his, pressing it flat so that she could feel the pounding of his heart under her touch.

"You okay?" he asked.

A slow smile curled her lips and she made a soft humming sound under her breath in response. "You know," she whispered, her voice all husky and rough, the way a woman sounded in the morning after a long night of hot, lazy sex. "I dreamed about you last night."

If he was a smart man, he'd get a little bit of distance between them, Blake thought. A little bit of distance so he could try to cool the fire in his gut because it was going to eat him alive. He didn't move an inch. "What kind of dream?"

Another one of those soft, sexy humming sounds and then Del leaned in closer, closer so he could feel all those hot, lush curves. "This kind." He could feel his grip on self control getting more and more tenuous. He clung to it with a sweaty, slippery grip and he wasn't sure how long he could take this.

Then Del slid her arms around his neck and slanted

her mouth over his. She kissed him, hard and deep, like she was as greedy as he was. It wasn't possible, Blake didn't think, but there was no mistaking the hunger in her kiss or the way she pressed her body against his. He could feel her breasts against his chest, the soft weight pressing flat, her nipples hard.

It was sweet, sweet torture and Blake knew he'd take it as long as he had to, so long as she didn't stop and he didn't scare her. Still, he had to touch her though. Just a little.

He brought one hand up, keeping the other fisted at his side. The short tank she wore had ridden up and when he laid his hand on her side, he touched bare, damp flesh. Involuntarily, he rolled his hips forward and for a brief second, he felt her against him. Her cotton pants clung like a second skin and he could feel her, all heat and softness. His hand flexed and he pumped against her a second time and then she went stiff against him.

She tore her mouth away from his and backed away. Her breath wheezed out of her lungs and her pupils were so damn big, the black almost eclipsed the soft green of her irises. That dazed, drugged hunger was gone and in its place, a naked fear.

"Del—" He started to reach for her, cussing himself ten different ways to Sunday as he stared at her pale face.

She shook her head. "Don't apologize, Blake." She closed her eyes and pressed her lips together. When she looked back at him, she didn't look so terrified, but the hungry woman from seconds ago was gone. "Please don't apologize."

"I scared you. Shit. I'm..."

"Don't say you're sorry," Del said quietly. "And you didn't scare me. At least, not you in particular. I don't want you to be sorry—I'm not."

He watched as she touched her lips. She looked at him and whispered, "You have no idea how long it's been since I've been able to let anybody do that." Then she laughed. "Well, maybe you do. The last time I allowed anybody get that close was that last day at the lake."

Shit. Blake didn't know if he was elated to hear that or terrified. Elated because it could maybe, just maybe, mean that she hadn't ever gotten over him either. Terrified for a couple of reasons. If he pushed too hard and screwed this up, he was going to leave even more scars on her and she had more than enough. Terrified because maybe what he had to offer her wasn't what she needed. Terrified that he'd scare her.

A smile flirted with her lips, like she knew what he was thinking. "Don't look so worried, Blake."

He felt completely helpless and like a total ass. "I scared you."

Del started to shake her head and then she stopped herself. "Yeah. A little. Maybe more than a little." She blew out a breath. "This isn't easy, you have to know that."

"I do." He took one slow step towards her, and then another. She watched him the same way a rabbit would watch a hawk, but she didn't pull away when he reached up to brush her hair back from her face.

She turned her face into his hand and pressed her lips against him. A knot lodged itself somewhere in the vicinity of his throat, making it damn near impossible to breathe as he stared at her. "So are you going to be okay if I want to do that again?" he asked.

Del's smile was there and gone, fast and fleeting. "Absolutely, I'm okay if you want to do it again." Then her face sobered. "But I come with a hell of a lot of baggage and even if I do want to try and move past this, I don't know if I'm ready for any kind of relationship. Even a casual one might be out of the question for me. I just don't know."

He cupped her chin in his palm and arched her face up, staring into her eyes. "I've never felt anything remotely casual for you, Del." When he kissed her this time, he kept his eyes open, watching her face. He kept the contact light and soft and then he stepped away. "I'm willing to take this as slow as you need, Del. I'll be patient and wait until you're ready. Only thing I'm not willing to do is let you walk away from me again. So if that's going to happen, maybe you'd better go ahead and do it now before this goes any farther."

Del cocked a brow at him. There was a faint ghost of her former confidence when she replied, "I'm not walking anywhere right now."

જ

Shit, shit, shit.

Del watched Blake's car until it turned the corner and disappeared from her line of sight and then she spun away from the open garage door. She touched her lips again and realized her hand was shaking.

It wasn't a big surprise—she felt about as solid and steady as a bowl of Jell-O.

I'm not walking anywhere.

The words had slipped out of her mouth before she really had time to think about them, but it was too late to take them back. With those words hovering between them, Del knew Blake would be back. He wasn't going to ask for anything she wasn't ready to give and she knew he'd be good as his word and wait.

Her fear was that she might not be ready. Not now. Not ever. Not soon enough for something to work out between her and Blake. Even without her history, it was a touch and go situation. She lived four hours away, she had a life, she had a job, an apartment—bills.

Okay, so she had more bills than she could afford to pay, a really shitty apartment and a job that she wasn't always sure she wanted. It wasn't exactly *home* but it was her life.

Prescott was what she thought of when she thought of *home*, but a long time had passed since she'd left. This was the home of her past, but she didn't know if she could live here again. She had made herself a life in Cincinnati.

Was she ready to change any of that? Could she change it?

஧

He wasn't going to kill him. Blake told himself that as he made the drive out to the country club. He was even fairly certain he meant it. He wasn't going to commit murder, as much as he wanted to.

The Pike County Country Club probably wouldn't add up to much in a more urban area, but around here, it was considered about as refined as it got. It wasn't exactly the good ole boys' club, but it wasn't too far off.

Blake didn't go there much. Once or twice a year, he might join his brother for a round of golf but that was about it. He had better things to do than sit around some smoke filled room and talk about how the interstate that bisected the county had just ruined everything. Better things to do than make "business" contacts, which struck him as ridiculous since he knew everybody in the damned county anyway.

But right now he wasn't there to play golf, or join the men for whiskey and cigars. He was heading for the golf course, but that was because it was Friday afternoon and every Friday afternoon, if the sun was shining and the temperature was above fifty degrees, William Sanders was on the golf course.

If Blake could have had his way, this would have been Sanders's last golf game, unless they played the game in hell. But the badge he wore was something he took seriously, something he had a hell of a lot of pride in. It was a bitch too. Legally, there was nothing anybody could do to William Sanders at this point.

The statute of limitations had come and gone twice over. The rape had been committed twelve years ago, and disgusting and awful as it was, Del wouldn't ever see justice over it.

But there was no way that Blake was going to let it go, not without putting the fear of God and himself into the sick bastard. And maybe, just maybe, William's temper and arrogance would get the better of him and the old bastard would take a swing at Blake. Wasn't an abuse of power if he was defending himself.

The sun shone down hot on his shoulders as he walked the course. He'd been offered a cart but he couldn't force himself into one. He had to move and he had to keep moving, because anytime he slowed down to think, that murderous rage threatened to take him over again.

Sanders was on the 11th tee with Cyrus Dougherty and Hank Teller. The three men saw Blake coming and Cyrus grinned. "Look, boys. Somebody called the sheriff on us. I told you we should have let them play through."

Blake had seen the teenagers who were waiting not so patiently for the older men to move along. Under normal circumstances, he might have played along. He'd always liked Cyrus. Cyrus owned the bank and the older man had given Blake the benefit of the doubt when he'd applied for the job in the sheriff's department.

But he wasn't in the mood for anything but blood. Not

being able to get it wasn't helping matters, either. "Need a word with you, Sanders," he said, keeping his voice level.

Sanders glanced up from his putt with a smile. "I'm pretty sure I paid Louisa's parking tickets."

Sanders showed no sign of hurrying so when Blake responded, he let a little bit of his rage enter his voice. "Nothing to do with parking tickets. Now, if you don't mind."

From the corner of his eye, Blake saw the other two eyeing him curiously, but he never took his gaze from Sanders as the older man straightened up. He held the putter out the caddy and headed towards Blake. "You want to tell me what this is all about?" William said. His voice was low and even but Blake saw the flash of irritation in his hazel eyes.

Blake smiled cynically and gestured. "You might want to take a walk with me, Sanders."

"I'm in the middle of a game. You can say whatever in the hell it is you need to say here," William replied.

Arrogant prick. Blake shrugged. "I figured you'd want a bit of privacy but if you don't mind your golf buddies knowing about how you raped—"

Those smug hazel eyes no longer looked so condescending and Blake grinned as William's face paled. He took off walking with a stiff gait and obliging, Blake fell in step behind him. He was nowhere near done with the audience yet, but he could let Sanders think whatever he wanted for the time being.

"What in the hell do you think you're doing, accusing

me of raping somebody?" William demanded. The brief walk had given him a minute to compose himself and when he looked back at Blake, he was as calm and collected as could be.

Blake knew better, though. He believed Dee, without a shadow of a doubt, but if he hadn't? Well, the guilty knowledge in William's eyes a few minutes ago would have erased any and all doubt. He smiled slowly. "Oh, I'm not accusing you of anything. I was just stating that you might like some privacy, unless you wanted your friends to know you raped your stepdaughter. You did want privacy, didn't you?"

William hung his head and sighed, a forlorn, sad sound that might have fooled a lot of people. Blake wasn't fooled, but he remained quiet as William looked at him and asked sadly, "Now what kind of tales has that girl of mine been telling you, Blake? She's had some trouble lately and she just can't admit her troubles are her own doing."

"I imagine she has had some troubles, considering what you did to her before she ran away."

William opened his mouth and Blake shook his head. "Don't. I ain't going to believe a damn word you say, so don't waste your breath." He moved closer, close enough that he could see Sanders's eyes widen, the pupils flare. The telltale nervous reaction satisfied some gut-deep, primitive need inside Blake. William Sanders was afraid. "And if you lie to me, Sanders, you're going to piss me off. You don't want me pissed off."

He watched as William swallowed nervously. It wasn't as good as beating him bloody and then using a rusty knife to cut the bastard's dick off, but fear was good. "You're going to stay away from Delilah, you understand me, Sanders?"

"She's my daughter—"

"No. She's nothing to you. She's not family, she's not a friend. She's not even a stranger you pass on the street," Blake said, keeping his voice soft and low. Then he reached out, grabbed a fistful of William's pale green polo shirt and jerked him close. "You don't talk to her, you hear me? You don't try to see her. Louisa decides she wants some sort of party, you talk her out of it. Not that Dee has any desire to see either of you, but even if she goes to the manor, you don't talk to her. You see her, you turn and go the other way."

He slowly loosened his grip. William stood there, frozen, almost as if he was afraid to move. Blake reached up and patted the old man's cheek once, twice—the third time he did it hard enough to sting and he heard the smack of flesh on flesh. A red imprint of his hand appeared William's cheek and the rest of his face darkened to match as a dull, ruddy flush crept up from his neck.

"I can't control what other people do, Blake."

"It's Deputy, Sanders. You best remember that. And you will control this, old man, because if you don't..." He leaned forward once more, put his mouth on level with William's ear. "If you don't, you're going to wake up one morning and find me standing over you. And it will be the last thing you see, because I'll kill you. Slow."

When he drew back, he saw that William's face had gone pale and his eyes were glassy. Satisfied he'd made his point, he turned and walked away.

Chapter Six

Two a.m. calls were never good.

Even for a deputy sheriff. Maybe even especially for a deputy sheriff. It was his weekend on call and he knew from experience any time that damn cell phone went off at this time of night it wasn't ever anything good.

He flipped open the phone and answered, "Mitchell," as he climbed from bed and grabbed the first pair of pants he saw. They happened to be the jeans he'd thrown on last night when he got home from work and they were wrinkled from laying in a heap on the ground, but at two a.m., people couldn't be picky about his attire.

Well, they could. He would just ignore them.

The voice on the other end of the line was that of Billy Darnell and although the deputy was decent in his job, he tended to be a little—dramatic. "Slow down and say that again," Blake interrupted and hoped that Billy's tendencies to exaggerate were playing into this.

Billy repeated himself and Blake figured that for once, the younger guy was actually sticking to the facts, which was bad, bad news. "I'm on my way."

He ended up behind the ambulance and judging by the way J.T. Amherst was driving, Billy had been right on the money about how serious the accident was. Lights from all of the vehicles shone on the wreckage, highlighting it all too well. Beaumont Junior drove a late model, sturdy SUV. A few months ago, he'd traded in a green Jaguar for the SUV. If he'd been driving the Jaguar, the paramedics wouldn't have to be so damned careful in their work because there wouldn't be anybody left to save.

As it was, Blake wasn't sure if all their valiant efforts were going to be worth much in the long run. The black oversized SUV had gone head-on with a big oak, but judging by the smashed up back end, Junior had some help going off the road.

He glanced at his watch and pressed a thumb and forefinger against his eyes. The call had gone into 911 less than fifteen minutes earlier when a nurse from County, Lizette Radcliff, drove past the wreckage on her way home from work. There weren't going to be any witnesses.

The medics started his way and Blake caught their attention. "He going to make it?"

J.T. glanced at him, his normally laughing eyes grim. "Don't know, Blake. He's lost a lot of blood. Took a bad blow to his head. Know more once we get him to the hospital."

Blake stood aside so they could do their job and as the ambulance went screaming off into the night, he turned back to the wreck and settled down to his.

Three hours later, Blake had a massive headache and

he was madder than hell. There was no question that somebody had run Junior off the road but that only left more questions and he didn't know if he'd find answers.

Who had done it?

Why had they left the scene?

There were other questions that Blake didn't want to think about but that was his job and he couldn't figure out which question was harder.

Was Junior going to make it through surgery?

Was this an accident—or intentional?

Blake couldn't quite shake the feeling that this hadn't been an accident. Logically, it could have been—kids out joyriding and not paying attention to the other vehicle until it too late, a drunk driver. There were other plausible explanations. But even though there was no evidence yet to indicate otherwise, nothing but a sick feeling in the pit of his gut. So if Junior died on the table, Blake and the rest of the sheriff's office were looking at a murder investigation. It wouldn't be the first murder in Prescott, or the last, but they weren't exactly commonplace. The last murder had been nearly ten years ago when Dawson Davis had come home early and found his bride of six months in bed with the next door neighbor.

Dawson's pretty bride got a divorce, the neighbor was six feet under and Dawson was doing hard time. Blake had been dealing with school and chemo but even he remembered that particular scandal. It had been the topic of conversation in Prescott for a good long while.

Dead tired, Blake closed his eyes and leaned back

against the wall. The waiting room of Pike County General was quiet this time of night. Junior's wife Marta was weeping softly in the corner, her sister holding her hand and staring at the doors with dazed eyes. In the other corner, their son sat with his head in his hands.

Samuel Wyatt Beaumont, III didn't look like either of his parents—he was big and rough looking next to his delicate, petite mother. Junior's hair had been gray as long as Blake had known him and every year, his hair receded just a little more. Sam, on the other hand, had thick hair that was as black as midnight and badly in need of a trim. He wore it long and usually tied back from his face but not tonight. The thick stubble on was normal, as were the dark clothes and beat up leather jacket.

He looked like a Hell's Angel. Maybe less scruffy, more clean shaven, and a lot younger, but he sure as hell didn't look like a lawyer. Very few would guess that the grim looking guy had attended an Ivy League college and graduated top of his class. Even harder to believe that he'd aced the bar exam and three years ago, he'd been a hotshot assistant district attorney down in Nashville. Something had changed, but Sam wouldn't talk about it with anybody, not even guys he used to call friend.

Now he drifted in and out of town, working odd jobs, disappearing at the drop of a hat without even picking up a paycheck. The past few weeks he'd been swinging a hammer, helping out with one of the rehabs going on in the older buildings down on the square.

Blake wasn't particularly looking forward to talking to Sam or his mother. Especially Sam. The man may look like a drifter but Blake knew the mind that lay behind those unreadable, brown eyes and if Sam suspected this hadn't been an accident, Blake was going to have even more trouble on his hands.

The doors opened and the four of them turned to watch as the doctor came inside. He had a weary smile on his face and the knots in Blake's gut eased.

"Looks like he's going to pull through. Those Beaumonts are stubborn."

"Is he awake?"

Dr. Joe Benson shook his head. "No. And when he does wake up, I'm not sure if he's going to be much help. He's got a pretty big knot on his head. He may not remember anything right away." Then Joe smiled ruefully. "Or ever."

Blake wasn't surprised, although he was frustrated, as he sat with Junior five hours later. The three of them weren't supposed to all be in the room at once. Junior had stabilized but he still didn't need the exhaustion of a lot of visitors. Blake had promised the doctor he'd keep it short and he figured the doctor knew better than to try and keep Sam and Marta away.

Blake glanced at his watch and told himself in two more minutes, he was going to leave. The last thing he wanted to do was add to Junior's exhaustion. "Okay, let's do this again, Junior. What's the last thing you remember?"

From across the room, Sam spoke up. "Why do you keep asking the same questions, Blake? Do you really think his answer is going to change from the last five times you asked?"

Marta had spent the past hour staring at Junior's face with a rapt gaze, as though she feared he might disappear in front of her. But when her son spoke, she glanced away from her husband. "Sam, darling, Blake is only doing his job. As long as he doesn't tire your father, Blake can ask the same question a thousand times. Whatever it takes to find who did this."

Junior laughed weakly. "I don't think a thousand times would make much difference, sweetheart." He lifted his wife's hand to his lips and kissed it before looking at Blake. Stooped shoulders lifted and fell as he sighed. "I can go over it again, but my answers won't change, Blake. I don't remember anything after I left the office. Not until I woke up here. I'm afraid I can't help you much."

Blake forced himself to smile. "That's understandable, Junior. What about before? Anything unusual happen in the office?"

"My word."

The four of them glanced to the door and Blake didn't quite manage to suppress his scowl as Louisa Sanders came sailing through the door. Behind her was the irritated face of the nurse taking care of Junior. She'd grudgingly let Blake in to see Junior, but she didn't look at all happy to have Louisa there.

"Mrs. Sanders, he needs to rest," Lena Ross said and judging by the irate tone of her voice, she'd said it several times.

"Oh come now, sweetie. I'm not going to keep him from resting. I just wanted to see how he was," Louisa said, waving a dismissive hand towards the nurse. She paused at the foot of the bed and touched a manicured hand to her throat. "Oh, dear Junior. I heard you were in an accident..."

"Mrs. Sanders, if you don't leave now I'm afraid I'll have to call security," the nurse warned.

Louisa's eyes flickered just a bit and she turned, giving the nurse a cool smile. "You'll do no such thing."

Lena's eyes widened. Temper flared there, but Blake had to give her credit. She kept her voice low and level as she said, "Mrs. Prescott, donating money to the pediatric wing doesn't make you exempt from hospital policy."

"Lena," Blake interrupted, drawing her attention to him. He doubted that Louisa could do much more than make petty threats but he didn't want to see her causing the nurse grief just for doing her job. "You don't need to call security. I'll handle this."

Lena paused and then she nodded. She left but at the door, he saw her glance back and give Louisa an irritated stare. As the door closed behind her, Blake stood up and said, "Why don't you let me walk you to the car?"

"Oh, don't be silly. I simply must see for myself that Junior is well." She edged around Blake and moved to stand beside the bed. She took Junior's hand in hers, squeezing gently. "Oh, Junior, we've all been so worried."

"Miz Sanders, you'll need to save your visiting for a different time," Blake said, his voice flat. "Junior got knocked around pretty good and—"

"Yes, so I heard," Louisa said, waving a hand. She looked at Marta, all but beaming. "I'm here to help in whatever way I can."

Marta smiled faintly. "Right now, we don't need anything, Louisa, but that is kind of you."

"Oh, don't be silly. Surely you could use a bite to eat. I'd be happy to sit with him while you two go down to the café for some lunch."

Blake stood up and closed the distance between them. He reached out and wrapped a hand around Louisa's upper arm, none too gently herding her to the door. "The nurses brought them food already. He's not on his deathbed and I doubt Marta needs anybody clucking around her like a mother hen. I'm in the middle of trying to figure out what happened so you will have to come back later." He stepped out in the hall, and just in case she decided to get ugly, he closed the door behind him.

If he didn't know the woman as well as he did, Blake wouldn't have seen the venom in her eyes. She covered it quickly, but he saw it nonetheless. "You will not touch me, Blake Mitchell," she said. The smile never left her face and she never raised her voice. In fact, ice all but dropped from each word.

"Your mistress to servant act might work on some people, but I'm not impressed. Go home, Louisa. Now."

He turned to go back inside, dismissing her. Louisa didn't much care for being dismissed, though. "Who do you think you are, speaking to me in such a manner?"

she demanded. "You think that badge of yours means you can do this?"

Blake let go of the doorknob and turned back to Louisa. He took his time with his answer, leaning up against the wall, pausing to brush off an invisible speck of lint from his shirt. "I think I'm investigating a hit and run that could have killed a man. That is a crime. And you, I believe, are interfering?" Something mean and ugly stirred inside of him and it showed in the smile he gave her. "Ever spent a couple hours behind bars, Louisa? After all, you are interfering with my investigation."

She drew back her shoulders and stared down her nose at him. "You wouldn't *dare*."

Blake shoved off the wall and bent down, putting his face level with hers. "You wanna bet?"

Louisa sneered. "I'd have your job before the end of the day."

"No." Blake shook his head. "You wouldn't. You won't do anything to get in my way, Louisa. If you do, people are going to hear about what you allowed your husband to do to your daughter. Why she left. She wasn't in some rich boarding school like you've been telling everybody. She ran away—because you let him rape her."

Louisa went white. Then red. Her hand came up and when she slapped him, Blake didn't bother moving or blocking it. "You're as sick as Delilah is, telling such ugly lies," she whispered.

He snorted and asked, "Have you been telling yourself it was a lie for so long that you actually believe it?"

The answer was there, in her eyes, and then it was gone. She didn't believe her own lies, which meant she knew what she'd allowed to happen. She knew, and she didn't care, so long as nobody found out. "I can't lock you up for what you let happen," Blake said. "Not now, although I would if I could. I can't lock him up, for the same reason. Too much time has passed. But mark my words, Louisa, you go near her again and the two of you will pay. Maybe I can't make you pay in the eyes of the law for what you did, for what you let happen, but there are other ways. And I'll find every damn one of them."

"You think you can threaten me?" she demanded, her voice low and furious. "You stupid son of a bitch. *Nobody* threatens me. I'll have your job, damn you."

Laughing, Blake said, "No, you won't. You don't want to cross me, Miz Sanders."

Her face went white. She sucked in a breath of air, glanced around as though to make sure nobody was near enough to hear them. "Nobody would believe you. Nobody would dare believe you over *me*."

"Come off it, Louisa. You're not as important as you think you are," Blake said, shaking his head. "And sure they'd believe me. I work in the Sheriff's office. How easy do you think it would be to prove you never sent Dee off to some fancy school? People hear you lied about the boarding school, it won't be much of a stretch to have them believing every word you say is a lie. Not everybody is as impressed with you as you would like to think, Louisa. Quite a few of them would be more than happy to believe the worst." He turned back to the door. "Now you

103

get the hell away from me before I decide to throw your ass in jail, just for the hell of it."

ॐ

Bastard, Louisa seethed as she strode towards the elevator and jammed the button for the main level. *Arrogant son of a bitch. Does he think he can get away with this?*

He couldn't. Nobody could treat her like this. Nobody. Louisa Monroe Prescott Sanders came from one of the finest families in the South. The Monroes had lived in this part of Tennessee since the early part of the 1800s. At twenty, she had accepted the proposal from Douglass Prescott, marrying into a family so important, they had a town named after them.

And that bastard thought he could treat her like that...all because her spoiled bitch of a daughter came back to town. Twitching her ass, turning her nose up at her family responsibilities—damn Delilah. The girl had always been far too much trouble.

This matter wasn't over, Louisa told herself. For now, she was going to keep quiet, but it wasn't over.

Nobody threatened her and got away with it.

Nobody.

ॐ

"You look like hell."

After less than four hours of sleep and fourteen hours on his feet, Blake was surprised he didn't look worse than hell. Deedee—no, she didn't want to be called that any more. If he hadn't understood the need to separate herself from the helpless girl she'd been, Blake wouldn't care how many times she corrected him.

But Del did need it. So Del was what he'd call her. He met her eyes over the gleaming white tiles that lined the hallway outside the ICU at County and smiled. "You look beautiful," he murmured.

And she did. She snorted and Blake pushed his weary body out of the chair, approaching her carefully, the same way he would a wild animal. A faint smile curved her lips as she watched him and she said softly, "I'm not going to run away screaming, Blake."

He smiled back as he reached out and pushed a stray strand of hair back from her face. "I didn't think you would." Well, he'd been pretty sure she wouldn't. He didn't say that though.

She turned her face into his hand and that simple gesture wrapped a fist around his heart. Then she closed the distance between them and leaned against him, for a just a minute, resting her forehead against his chest. Unsure of what to do, but desperate to touch her, Blake cupped a hand around the back of her neck and dipped his head to kiss the top of her head.

She turned her face into him and Blake could have sworn she was smelling him. If he hadn't been thinking about burying his face in her neck to do the same thing, it might have been a little embarrassing. Instead, Blake felt some nameless, sappy emotion roll through him and he realized he felt more whole now than he'd felt in his entire adult life.

The last time he'd felt complete like this had been those few brief days they'd had together before the summer she disappeared from his life.

"You think awful loud," Del murmured. She nuzzled the front of his shirt and then stepped back, tucking her hands into her back pockets as she turned away. "I heard about Beaumont Junior. Is he going to be okay?"

Blake sighed and reached up a hand, running it along the smooth surface of his scalp. Belatedly, he realized he hadn't put a bandanna on and for some odd reason, he felt self conscious. To distract himself, he sat back down and picked up the report he'd been reading. Not that he'd find anything new there. "Should be fine. Going to be a while before he heals up though." He forced a smile. "Hope you don't need a lawyer any time soon. Junior's the only one I trust."

He glanced up at her and saw a thoughtful look on her face. "What is it?"

Del shook her head. "Nothing that can't wait, I imagine. I was supposed to go by Junior's and talk to him. Don't know what it was about. Manda gave me the message and I didn't get in touch with him yesterday."

She smiled at him. He felt a flush stain his cheeks red as she sauntered up to him and passed her hand, quick and light, over his head. "Damn, Blake. I never would have thought the cue ball look could be so sexy."

A grown man shouldn't blush as easy as that, Blake thought. He gave her a dirty look and focused on his report but Del apparently was in a talkative mood. "Look at you, blushing like that."

Grinning up into her soft green eyes, he teased, "Look at you, flirting like that. Smiling, even."

Del realized with a start that she had been flirting. She fell silent and an uncomfortable tension filled the air. Blake scowled and rubbed a hand over his face. "Del, I'm..."

She glared at him. "Would you stop apologizing so much?"

"I made you uncomfortable." And judging by the expression on his face, he wanted to kick himself.

Sighing, Del sat down beside him. Part of her wanted to press her body to his and just hold him. He looked exhausted and pissed off. She wasn't ready to touch him again just yet. The simple act of sitting there, feeling the warmth of his body so close to hers, the muscled line of his leg pressed snug against hers, was enough to have her internal radar shrieking out an alarm. "You didn't make me uncomfortable, Blake. Not really." She slid him a grin and added, "I guess I surprised myself. I didn't think I even remembered how to flirt."

For a minute, she thought he was going to remain all somber and serious. Damn it, she sucked at this. But then, he smiled, his eyes crinkling up at the corners as a grin lit his face.

"Feel free to practice on me as often as you want."

She bumped her shoulder against his. "I'll keep that in mind." Then she glanced at the clock. It was nearly five. "Are you going to be able to attend the reunion or does duty continue to call?"

"Shit." Leaning back, Blake closed his eyes.

"You forgot."

"I forgot."

With a shrug, she said, "If you don't want to go, it's not like people wouldn't understand."

"I do want to go." Then his eyes opened and he pinned her with a direct stare. "You're going, right?"

Del rolled her eyes. "If I don't, Manda will never forgive me."

"Then I want to go." He reached out his hand and Del laid her palm in his, linking their fingers. "Will you dance with me?"

She cocked a brow. "Now?" She glanced up and down the hallway, at the quiet nurses sitting at the nursing station outside the ICU and the doctors and hospital staff that carried on conversations in hushed voices. "The nurses probably wouldn't like it."

Blake grinned. The sight of that grin, his teeth flashing white against his deeply tanned skin, made her heart skip a beat or three. "I meant tonight, goofy."

Goofy...She squeezed his hand and murmured, "Yeah. I'd like that." She hadn't danced in years. Shoot, she hadn't wanted to dance in years and she hadn't wanted to flirt in years. She hadn't joked in years. Impulsively, she leaned in and kissed him on his smiling mouth. "I'm glad I came back, Blake."

She would have pulled away just as quickly, but he reached up with his free hand, cupping her face. He kept his touch light, so light and gentle she could have pulled away if she wanted, but she felt as though she'd been frozen in place. She held still as he leaned in and pressed his mouth to hers. It wasn't quick and light. It was slow, it was thorough and it was devastating. He traced the contour of her lips with his tongue, sucked her lower lip into his mouth. When he would have pulled away, she curled a hand into his shirtfront and held him close as she opened her mouth for him.

He groaned against her lips and then slanted his mouth across hers, deepening the kiss. He pushed his tongue into her mouth and Del bit him, quick and light, before sucking on him, pulling him deeper. Damn, the way he tasted...it was addictive. It was the burn of whiskey, the silken smoothness of good vodka and as sweet as sin.

It was the kind of taste a woman could come to crave. Del had fought long and hard to work past craving anything but this was a sweet temptation that she didn't want to resist. Slowly, unnerved by the strength of her need, she pulled back.

Lifting her lashes, she stared at him. His lids drooped low over his eyes as he rubbed his thumb across her lower lip. "I'm glad you came back, too, baby."

Chapter Seven

"I can't wear this," Del muttered, staring at her reflection and panicking. She didn't own too many dresses. She had bought the plain black dress for job interviews back when she'd graduated and it was the closest thing to formal she owned.

It was also as ugly as hell.

She grabbed her hair into a loose ponytail, pulling it up off her neck and hoping that would help. Even worse, now people could see the shoulders of the dress. Maybe a necklace—

No. That wouldn't help either.

"Oh, hell." She walked over to the bed and flopped face down on it with a groan.

"What's wrong?"

Lifting her head, Del stared at Manda through her hair. "Everything."

She rolled off the bed and went to stand in front of the mirror again, groaning at her reflection.

Manda bit her lip to keep from smiling. "Now come on, sweetie. Not everything is wrong." She studied the dress and then said, "That dress is seriously wrong. But not everything. Hmmmm..." She propped one hand on her hip and studied Del closely. She tapped a fingernail painted a pretty coral against her lips. Then she reached out and grabbed Del's hand. "Come on."

"Come where?"

"We're going to find you something decent to wear."

Del glanced at Manda's reed-thin figure and then down at her rather substantial chest. "Honey, I can't fit into anything you own."

"Not me. My cousin Sarah bought the *Boutique on the Square* when Evvie died last year. She doesn't close until six."

"It's twenty 'til six."

Manda waved a hand. "I'll call her on the way. She owes me big time, anyway. She can either do this...or baby sit. Believe me, she'd rather do this."

Del continued to drag her heels. "I don't know, Manda..." Even as much as she hated the way she looked in this ugly dress, Del didn't know if she was ready to try wearing something that *wasn't* plain, utilitarian just plain ugly or all three.

The reunion dinner wasn't exactly a formal affair, but dressing up for anything just wasn't her. Trying to look nice wasn't her.

At least not any more. She remembered the girl she'd been, closets full of expensive, pretty clothes, and boxes upon boxes of shoes. She didn't miss that girl at all. But as she thought about all of the clothes she used to wear, she thought of the dances she'd been to with Blake and she remembered the look on his face when he'd seen her the night he picked her up for their first formal.

It had been for a dinner dance at the country club and she'd gone into Nashville to buy her dress. She'd loved that dress. It had been nearly the same green as her eyes with skinny, sparkling straps covered with rhinestones. It was cut slim and if it hadn't been for the slit on the side on either knee, walking would have been a chore.

She'd looked gorgeous. Del hadn't been a vain girl— she had loved fun, pretty clothes, loved all the fussy, female things that came with being a girl, but she hadn't really been vain. Confident, maybe. Thinking back to that night, she knew that she'd looked good—and Blake had thought so too.

Grimly, she looked down at the black shapeless thing she now wore. Then she gave Manda a hard smile. "Come on. Let's go."

ৡට

Standing by the bar, a beer in one hand and the other jammed deep into his pocket, Blake wondered if maybe he shouldn't just go on home. He was so tired he ached with it and his eyes were gritty with fatigue.

It had been a shitty day. Junior was still holding his own although the doctors were keeping him sedated to keep him from feeling the pain from his numerous injuries.

So far, no witnesses had stepped up and the only real evidence they had was some paint on the bumper of Junior's SUV. Now if Blake could just go and check out every black car in the county, he might be able to find who'd run Junior off the road.

"You're not really here tonight, are you, buddy?"

He looked up at Vance and forced a smile. "Just tired. One hell of a day."

Vance nodded. "Yeah, I heard you were there with Junior last night. Hope the old guy is going to be okay. You remember back when..." Vance started rambling about one of the many times the two of them had gotten into trouble their senior year and Blake just tuned him out, thinking, again about Del.

"Damn, there you go again."

Vance's voice, louder this time, intruded on Blake's introspective thoughts and Blake winced. "Sorry, man. My mind is just wandering."

"Yeah...I noticed...whoa."

Blake watched as Vance's jaw dropped and his eyes went wide. He was staring off over Blake's shoulder and curious, Blake glanced back, following Vance's line of sight.

His beer bottle fell from numb hands as he turned to stare at Del. Or at least, he was pretty damn sure it was Del. Her hair, still dark, was scooped up off of her neck and clipped to her head in one of those tousled styles that made a guy think just how easy it would be to send all

113

those gleaming locks tumbling to her shoulders. Her naked shoulders. She was wearing a pale green dress, a dress that Blake knew would match her eyes perfectly. It was off the shoulder, with long sleeves that went all the way to her wrists. The dress skimmed her curves closely and Blake felt his mouth go dry as he stared at those curves with hungry eyes. The skirt fell in soft folds to just above her knee. And her pretty little feet were stuck into a pair of strappy, sparkly heels that did amazing things for her already amazing legs.

"Damn."

Vance laughed and clapped his hand on Blake's shoulder. "Yeah, I can see now why you weren't paying me any attention," Vance said as Del met his eyes from across the room. A faint smile curved her lips up and she walked towards him.

Blake started over to meet her, but Vance's hand tightened. Looking back at Vance, he saw a serious look had come over Vance's face. "Be careful, okay, Blake? She's had a rough time."

If it was anybody other than Vance, discussing anybody other than Del, he would have told him to mind his own business. But with Vance, all he did was nod and say, "I know."

Blake had every intention of being very damn careful because there was no way he could let Del go. Not now.

Although she still had that same hold over him that she'd always had, the woman moving towards him was definitely different. The smile on her lips wasn't the flirtatious, sexy smile he remembered. It was a cool, confident smile, yet the look in her eyes was almost hesitant.

He closed the distance between them and used the time to try and clear his head. It didn't work. The need flowing through him had been building inside him for years. This was the girl he'd loved for nearly half his life, the girl he'd wanted more than anything. Seeing her like this just about laid him low.

They came to a stop just shy of touching. "Hey." He tried to find something funny to say, something that might make that faint, half-smile on her face bloom into a real one. But nothing came to mind except, "Shit, you look amazing."

Hardly funny or charming, but it must have been good enough for her. Her smile turned self-conscious and she ducked her head shyly, tucking a stray lock of hair behind her ear. Then she slid her gaze over him and murmured, "You too. You look damn good. considering the fact that you didn't sleep more than three or four hours last night."

She looked back up at him and cocked her head. A couple of long, shiny strands of hair fell loose from the clip, framing her face just so, teasing her neck and shoulders. Blake wanted to tear the clip away, see all that long, dark hair fall around her shoulders and then he wanted to bury his hands in it and kiss her. Instead, he shoved his hands in his pockets so he wouldn't reach for her. She asked, "How's Beaumont Junior doing?"

"Hanging in there." He gave her a humorless smile. "Had the pleasure of your mama's company for a few minutes. She came by to cluck over Beaumont and fulfill her duty as the gracious lady of the manor routine."

Del grimaced. "That's my mother. Doesn't miss an opportunity to put on her pretenses."

She fidgeted with her dress and unable to stop himself, Blake reached out and caught one of her hands, lifting it to his lips. "You look gorgeous."

He kissed her hand, watching her from under the fringe of lashes. A soft blush stained her cheeks pink, her cheeks, her neck...lower. He found himself staring at the neckline of her dress and he tore his gaze away as he realized he was ogling her breasts. He wanted to do more than ogle. He wanted to peel the dress off and lick her all over. Instead, he gestured to the dance floor. "You know, I never got to dance with you at my senior prom. Why don't you make it up to me now?"

The smile that curved her lips up hit in the chest with the force of sledgehammer.

"I'd love to."

He led her out onto the dance floor and guided her hands, first one, then the other up to his shoulders. From the speakers, Garth Brooks sang a song about unanswered prayers. Blake wasn't much for praying. Back before he'd stopped asking God for anything, though, this had been a regular prayer—having this woman back in his arms.

Maybe unanswered prayers weren't the only thing to

thank God for. At that moment, Blake was grateful for the answer to a prayer that had been a long time coming. Del moved against him awkwardly at first, her body tense, but bit by bit, she relaxed.

"So did you miss me at your senior prom?" she asked, cuddling against him just like she used to.

Lowering his head, he brushed a kiss against her cheek. He breathed in the soft, warm scent of her and managed to stifle his moan—just barely. His voice was hoarse as he told her, "Not a bit."

Tipping her head back, she asked, "Not even a little?"

"Nope." Then he smiled and confessed, "I didn't go." Cupping a hand over the back of her head, he eased her back against him. "Wasn't interested."

Through the thin silk of her dress, he could feel the heat of her body and it was killing him. He could feel the soft, sweet weight of her breasts, the flat planes of her belly. His left hand rested at the small of her back and he was almost painfully aware of the rounded curve of her ass. Nuzzling her neck, he murmured, "Did you miss your prom?"

Against his chest, Del smiled. "I missed half of my junior year and almost all of my senior year. The only prom I went to was your junior prom."

Blake stroked a hand up her back. "Then we have quite a few dances to catch up, don't we? You think you can close your eyes and pretend you're wearing some sexy little formal number and I've got my James Bond attire on? We can pretend there's some half-assed wedding-type band on the stage and we're going to dance just a few dances before we slip out to find someplace to go neck."

"Hmmmm." Her gaze dropped to his lips. "Necking, huh?"

"Yeah. Remember that junior prom? You had a pretty green dress on. Almost the same color as your eyes."

She laughed. "That wasn't the prom, sugar. It was the dinner dance at the country club."

He shrugged. "Prom. Dinner dance. I had to wear a monkey suit for both of them, but it was worth it to see you. If the green dress was the dinner dance, then that pink number—it was the prom, right?"

Del nodded. The pink number, as Blake called it, had been a designer dress she'd bought from a boutique in Lexington. Her breath hitched a little as she remembered that night. He'd peeled her out of her dress and if a county sheriff hadn't shown up, he would have had her out of the strapless bra and her panties before too long.

He cupped the back of her head, arching her head up to look at him. His lids were low, giving him a sleepy-eyed look as he murmured, "Yeah, that was prom, all right." A wicked light entered his eyes. "That was the night I got to see the princess of Prescott wearing nothing but a lacy pink bra and lacy pink panties."

She felt her face burn and knew she must be blushing to the roots of her hair. "That was the night you stole those pink lace panties and wouldn't give them back."

He grinned at her and bent down, pressing a quick, light kiss to her lips that set her blood to a slow boil.

"Yeah...you're right." Pressing his lips to her ear, Blake murmured, "Can I tell you a secret...I still have them."

A startled, embarrassed laugh escaped her. "You do not." Then she pulled away and looked at him. "Do you?"

With a grin crooking his lips, he shrugged. "That's kind of a pathetic thing to lie about, holding on to some pink silk panties for more than twelve years." He brushed his fingers across her lower lip. "I also kept all the letters you sent me that summer while I was gone." A harsh look tightened his face and he glanced around.

He grabbed her hand and guided her off the dance floor and out the open doors that led to the patio. It wasn't much quieter out there and he led her past the groups of laughing people into the gardens just beyond. It was darker out there, away from the lights of the patio, and quieter. From there, the sounds of the music were distant and faint.

"I wish you would have said something, Dee—Del," he corrected himself.

She pressed a fingertip to his lips. "You can call me whatever you want, Blake."

He caught her hand in his wrist and pressed a kiss to her palm. "I kept those letters, Dee. I've read them so many times they're practically falling apart. Why didn't you say something?"

"I didn't know what to say," she responded. She gently tugged her hand away from his, then reached up, cupped his neck, tugging him closer. He dipped his head and she rose onto her toes, kissing him softly. "I wanted to say something. But I was too afraid. Too ashamed."

Tears burned her eyes and Blake swore softly. Bending his head, he kissed her eyes. "Don't cry," he pleaded. "Please, don't cry."

He kissed her lips and she sighed into his mouth. He'd meant to make her feel better, that was all. She knew that. But it went from comforting to seductive in the span of heartbeats. His hands wrapped around her body, pulling her close and she groaned, arching into him. She wrapped her arms around his neck and clung tight, opening her mouth to his and whimpering with pleasure as he pushed his tongue into her mouth.

Against her breasts, she could feel that hard muscled wall of his chest, and the rapid beat of his heart. His hands roamed restlessly over her back and Del knew that he wanted more. Needed it—she could feel the hunger raging inside him and surprisingly, she felt it echoed in her own body. Damn it, she needed him.

There were nights she'd lain awake, unable to sleep, so sick and lonely inside it hurt. She'd think of him, remember who she'd been before her life had fallen apart. Happy, innocent—and his. She'd wished, so often, that she could go back to being that girl.

But she'd accepted a long time ago that there was no turning back the clock, that she and Blake just weren't meant to be.

Now, though, she had a chance. Not at turning back the clock—she couldn't go back to the innocent girl she'd been, but she could be his.

He wanted her—it was in the desperate, hungry way he kissed her and the way his hands roamed over her body like he couldn't touch her enough. She could be his—and in that moment, she knew why she'd never been able to get close to the few men who had tried over the years. She couldn't get close because she still belonged to Blake, heart and soul.

She wanted more than that now—she needed to belong to him completely. Heart, soul and body. Pulling her head back, she looked up into his eyes. "I want you to take me home, Blake."

He swore raggedly. "Damn it, Del. I'm sorry. I'm moving too fast here."

Blake turned away and she reached out, grabbed his wrist. Under her fingertips, she felt the erratic beat of his pulse. It was beating as fast as her own. "No, Blake. I want you to take me to your home."

Slowly, holding his gaze with hers, she tugged him back to her and then she slid her hands inside the black blazer he wore. She curved her hands over his narrow waist and tugged his lower body into close contact with hers. "I want you to make love to me."

A harsh breath hissed out of him as he cupped her face in his hands. His eyes, dark with need, searched her face. "Damn it, Dee. Are you sure?" His hands were shaking, she realized.

Confidence surged inside her. He wanted her so much that he was shaking with it. And still—he was careful not to rush her. In response, she turned her head and pressed his lips to his hand. Opening her lips, she nipped his palm. "I've never been more sure of anything in my life." A deep sense of honesty had her admitting, "That doesn't mean I can promise you I won't freak out, but I want to try."

He slid his hands into her hair, arching her head back and gazing down into her eyes. He bent his head, kissing her gently. "All you have to do is say the word, baby, and I'll stop."

"I know that. I'm just hoping I won't get scared enough to make you."

Instead of going back into the country club, they took one of the garden paths back around to the parking lot. Neither of them said a word. The silence between them was taut with tension, but it wasn't uncomfortable. Del felt the searing heat of his gaze as he opened the door to his car. He held her hand while she climbed inside but instead of closing the door right away, he leaned in and took the seat belt from her, strapping her in. Bent over, his mouth was on level with her neck. Unable to resist, he leaned forward and pressed his lips to her neck.

When he placed his hand on her belly, she jumped. He eased back, looking into her eyes. "You okay?"

Del swallowed around the knot in her throat and nodded.

Sliding his hand upward, he cupped her breast. "You got no idea how many times I dreamed about just this," he said, his voice hoarse.

Terrified and excited all at once, Del forced herself to

smile. "No. Probably not. I stopped letting myself dream a long time ago." She arched into his hand and moaned when he circled his thumb around her nipple. "But I bet I missed out on a lot of really good dreams starring you."

A burst of raucous laughter rang through the night and they pulled away, slowly. A couple of ex-football players came tearing by, one of them holding a worn old ball tucked under his arm and two others running like mad to catch him.

"Let's get out of here."

ò

As he turned off the car's ignition, Blake saw his hands were shaking. He glanced at Del's face and saw her staring at the lake house with a look of bemusement. "I still live at the house with Mama. Had an apartment while I was in college but then I got sick..." His voice trailed off and he felt like an idiot, explaining that he hadn't ever left home. "By the time the doctors decided I was in remission, Mama got sick and...well, she needed me."

She gazed at him, a smile on her mouth. "That's sweet, Blake." She touched the pad of her finger against his lower lip and asked, "You think I care if you live at home with your mom or not? I adore your mother."

"Yeah. Me too. But I don't want to take to Bel Rive right now." He didn't want to go any place where he might have to share even five seconds of her attention. And he had no doubt that his mother would know if he brought

Del home. She'd know—and come morning, she'd want them both down at breakfast and knowing Angel, she'd be working on wedding plans.

He wasn't opposed to planning a wedding, but it might be best to see how Del felt about it first.

He climbed from the car and tried to use the next few seconds to clear his head and level out. God knew the last thing Blake wanted was to scare Del. Hurt her. Upset her in any way. But he was so damned desperate for her, he didn't trust himself to stay in control.

You have to, he told himself as he opened the door and took her hand to help her out. She laid her hand in his and climbed from the car. Then, with a smile, she closed the distance between them and pressed her body to his. "You used to bring me out here to make out."

He glanced at the cabin his great grandfather had built a good forty years before he'd been born. Each generation had built onto it and Blake was in the slow process of expanding the deck so he could put in a hot tub. "Did I really?" Not that he had forgotten. There had been times when he hadn't come to the lake house more than once or twice a year just because the memories he had of Dee here had been enough to turn his gut into knots. "Maybe you should refresh my memory. I don't recall that."

She laughed and slid her arms around his neck. "Hmmm. Is that so?" She pressed her lips to his. Blake fisted his hands to keep from grabbing her as she traced the line of his mouth with her tongue. He opened for her and she kissed him deeper. Through their clothes, he felt her body shudder and she moaned. The sound of that hungry female moan hit him, low and hard.

"Remember yet?"

"Not a bit," he lied. He pulled his hands out of his pockets slowly, slid them around her waist. He watched her face, looking for some sign of fear or worry, but all he saw was an echo of the hunger he felt inside.

"Maybe you should take me inside then. I'll see if I can't refresh your memory a little better."

Bending his knees, he slid an arm under her legs and scooped her up into his arms. "Might not be a bad idea."

She smiled at him. "You still got that old couch in the game room? We could try there, see if that doesn't tickle some memory."

Blake shook his head. "No. Got rid of that a while back. Don't worry—I've got something better." The night was cool and he knew exactly where he wanted her. In his room, with the windows open so the breeze from the lake would drift in while he stripped her naked and laid her on his bed.

It took a little bit of work to unlock the door with her in his arms, but she didn't seem in any hurry to let go of him and Blake sure as hell had no desire to let go of her. He finally managed to get it open and he kicked it shut behind him before carrying her up the stairs to the newest addition to the lake house. His room faced out over the lake and had a series of French doors that could be opened in cooler weather. Lowering her to her feet he flicked on the light and then he went and opened each of the three French doors, letting the breeze in.

It drifted in, making the mosquito netting that draped over the bed billow. "I love coming out here on nights like this, sleeping with the doors open." He led her to the bed and brushed the netting aside before he picked her up and put her down on the mattress. "I've had a million dreams like this, of you coming back home, coming back to me. I'd bring you and make love to you on this bed."

Kneeling beside her, he placed his hand on the soft, delicate curve of her belly and he murmured, "I didn't ever expect it to happen though."

She reached up, pressed her hand to his cheek. He turned his head, kissing her palm. "Nothing has to happen," he whispered, looking back at her. "If you want me to stop, just say it. I will."

Del smiled and slid her hand around the back of his neck, tugging him down to her. "I know. But I don't want to think about that. Kiss me, Blake. I always loved it when you kissed me."

Kissing was good, he thought, stretching out beside her. He covered her mouth with his, keeping the contact light and easy. He kept his hand on her belly, rubbing in slow circles that went ever higher. When he reached her breasts, he stilled, waiting for her to pull away but she didn't. No, Del caught his hand and urged him closer, so that he cupped her breast in his hand.

Damn. She was so soft. Under his thumb, her nipple was hard and stiff and Blake pulled away, scooting down on the bed so he could take her nipple into his mouth. He didn't cover her body with his the way he wanted to—and damn, did he want to. He wanted to strip her naked, cover her and push into her, taking her hard and fast. Instead, he kept his weight off of her as he bit down gently on her nipple.

She groaned and arched closer cradling his head in her hand. She clung to him, like she needed to feel him closer. *Slow...easy...*he told himself as he smoothed a hand down her hip and then around, up her back until he found the zipper of her dress. He tugged on it, pulling it down just an inch as he looked up at her. "Don't suppose we could lose this dress, could we?"

She sat up, reaching behind her for the zipper and he caught her hands gently, bringing them back to her lap before he moved around behind her. "Let me," he murmured, dragging the zipper down slowly. As the material parted, it exposed soft, pale flesh. Blake dipped his head, pressing a kiss to her naked back.

She wiggled a little, pulling her arms out of the sleeves. Looking over her shoulder at him, she smiled and lifted her arms. He didn't realize what she was doing until her bra fell away. She lay back down and Blake's mouth went dry as he stared at her.

Her breasts—damn it, how could she look more perfect than she had back when they were kids? Didn't seem possible, but there you go.

Her breasts were big. They had always filled his hands to overflowing and that hadn't changed a bit. Her nipples, tight pink buds, caught his attention and he groaned. He wanted to ravage. Wanted to feast on the soft white flesh and gorge himself on her. But instead, he lay on his back, tugging her hands until she came to her knees.

"Come here," he said hoarsely, guiding her so that she straddled him, one leg on either side of his hips.

It put her on the perfect level for him to take one plump, pert nipple into his mouth, licking, stroking and suckling until she was rocking against him and moaning his name.

Then he switched his attention to the other one. Smoothing his hands down over her hips, he caught the skirt of her dress and pushed it up. The bodice still hung around her waist and now, with her skirt pushed up, he could see almost every, sweet, perfect inch of her. "Sit up," he told her, pulling back. "I need to see you."

She sat up slowly and he studied her, her swollen pink mouth, her breasts, soft, white and round rising with each ragged breath. "You're still overdressed."

Del grinned at him and tugged on his lapels. "You're wearing more than me."

Blake caught her hands and kissed them. "Self preservation. I'm holding onto my control by the skin of my teeth."

Her grin faded, replaced a shy, almost nervous smile that just about broke his heart. "I'm okay, Blake. I swear. Part of me feels like I've been waiting for this my whole life." She bent over him and kissed him and it was every bit as desperate and hungry as he felt inside. "Don't make us wait any longer."

"I don't want to scare you."

She wiggled on top of him and his eyes crossed as he felt the heat and moisture of her through the layers of clothing. "I don't think scared describes how I feel right now."

Then, holding his gaze, she stood up on the bed. It was canopy styled bed but instead of a fabric canopy, it had scrolled metal that crossed at the center in an X, with the mosquito netting draped over the X. She wrapped her hands around two legs of the X and wiggled her hips. The skirt fell in a silken puddle to her feet, forgotten. Reaching up, she grabbed the clip from her hair and pulled it out. The long, razor-straight tresses fell down to frame her face, falling around her shoulders, the ends of her hair flirting with her nipples.

"Oh, shit," Blake swore roughly. She was wearing a tiny pair of lacy green underwear. It was cut a little different from a bikini, fuller, and covering more of her hips. But it dipped low, and he meant *low* over her belly and as he slowly sat up, he caught a glimpse of her ass. The lace rode high on her butt, clinging to each round curve with devotion. Rolling to his knees, he cupped her buttocks in his hands, tugging her closer. He pressed his mouth to her and above him, Del cried out, a sharp, startled sound.

Quickly, he lifted his head and looked at her. "You okay?"

Her eyes were wide and glazed. Her breath came in

ragged pants as she murmured, "Oh, I'm fantastic."

Blake chuckled. "You're not kidding." Then he glanced upward to the metalwork over her head. "Hold on tight, baby girl." Pulling her close, he pressed his mouth more fully against her, kissing her through the silk. It was wet—already drenched from her. He groaned and reached between her legs to push the silk aside so he could taste her better.

Above him, Del whimpered. "Oh, damn."

Despite himself, he grinned. He licked her clit and she shuddered. He circled it with his tongue and she jerked against him. Her hands came down from the metalwork over the bed and slammed against his shoulders. He lifted up just a little and she made a soft sobbing sound in her throat and curved a hand over the back of his head, trying to draw him close, once more.

She didn't need to ask twice. He leaned back in and this time, he pressed his mouth more firmly against her. Slowly, he circled his tongue around her clit. The hand she had around the back of his head tightened and she rocked against him. Those frantic, greedy motions added to the fire burning inside him and he growled triumphantly.

Blake stroked his hands down her hip, pushing her panties down until they fell around her ankles. She stepped out of them, wobbled a little and put her foot down fast, widening her stance on the bed.

"Shit, are you trying to kill me?" he demanded, staring at the pink, wet folds of her sex.

He laid one hand on her thigh and sat back on his heels, watching her face as he cupped her sex "You're the sweetest damn thing." Slowly, he pushed one finger inside her, slowly. Very slowly, watching the expression on her face.

It was amazing—her lids fluttered down. Her mouth fell open and she sighed out his name. He pumped his finger inside her, once, twice. She looked down at him, her hair falling around her shoulders and into her face. The ends of it reached her chest, so dark against the pink and white of her breasts. His mouth watered and he took her again, using his lips, his tongue and his teeth on her. He continued to pump his finger inside her, stroking deep. As the slick, wet tissues of her sex started to tighten around him, he pushed deeper—pressing against a spot inside her sheath.

Del came. Her body sagged against him and he supported her weight as she screamed out his name. Bracing his forearm at her hips, he struggled to keep her balanced as she rocked against his mouth, her pussy clenching around his fingers, and his name falling from her lips in a startled scream.

Slowly, he pulled away, pulling his finger from the tight, silky clasp of her sex. Cupping her bottom in his hands, he eased her down, her body sliding against his. He kissed the tip of one breast, licked a path upward, raked his teeth against her neck. She settled against his lap, her arms draped around his shoulders. Her face flushed as she stared at him. "Uhhhmmm." She ducked her head, buried her face against his shoulder.

"Damn it, you're sweet." He nuzzled her hair.

"Whatever." Squirming in his lap, she lifted her head, tugged at the jacket he wore. "You're still overdressed."

He chuckled and pressed a kiss to her mouth. She stiffened and he lifted his head, staring at her. "Open up for me, Del. I need more."

"You're too damn hard to say no to," she whispered, leaning in and pressing her lips to his.

Cradling her head in his hands, he kissed her slowly, pushing his tongue into her mouth. Slowly, teasingly. Then he lifted his head and rasped, "See how sweet you are?"

The corners of her mouth twitched in a smile. "And you're still overdressed."

"Then why don't you do something about it?"

She cocked a brow. "Good question." She squirmed backwards and settled on her knees in front of him. "Nice jacket," she said as she stripped it off.

"Thanks." He dropped his gaze to her naked body and reached out, cupping her in his hand. "Nice—" He grinned wolfishly as her gaze flew up to meet him. "Nice everything."

"I can't take your shirt off if you don't be still."

Obligingly, he pulled his hand back and held motionless as she undid the row of ebony buttons marching down the front of his shirt. "How can you look even better now than you did high school?" she muttered, staring at his chest as she pushed his shirt off his shoulders.

Blake shrugged out of it and tossed off to the side. "I was wondering the same thing about you."

She grinned at him. "Really." She swayed forward, licked his lips and then looked down, watched as she rested her hands on his thighs. His muscles jerked under her touch and she glanced upward. She undid his belt, loosened the button on the black linen pants and then dragged the zipper down. Her voice shook as she murmured, "You'll need to move."

Although she didn't look away from him, although she didn't say anything, Blake saw the nervous fear darkening her eyes. He leaned forward and kissed her gently before easing back off the bed, shoving the netting out of this way. He finished the job, shoving his pants and the black boxer briefs down at the same time. His cock bobbed against his belly as he straightened and the cool brush of air against his rigid flesh was almost painful. He needed to be inside her, wrapped in the sweet satin of her pussy but he held still, waiting for her.

She stared at him, her eyes rapt on his face. She swallowed and he said softly, "Just tell me you've changed your mind, Del. I'll live through it." He grimaced and glanced down at his throbbing length. It would be painful as hell but he'd survive. He'd never forgive himself if he scared her.

"You might," she said, her voice shaking. "But would I?" She sank back and stroked a hand down the bed. "Lay down."

He came back to the bed and the white mosquito netting fell back around the bed. The gauzy cloth softened the light and he gazed at Del as he lay down, hardly able to believe how beautiful she looked in the misty, golden light filtering through the netting. She leaned over him, bracing her hands against his chest as she straddled his hips.

He groaned as she rubbed against him, wet, hot silk. She dipped her head and he reached up, caught her chin. "Look at me, Del. I haven't waited this long for you to hide away the first time we make love," he rasped. "Not in any way. Look at me."

She lifted her head and their gazes locked and held. "You do it, Del. If you want this, you do it."

*Well, put that way...*Del hissed out a nervous breath. Yes, she wanted this. She wanted Blake so bad it hurt inside. A hard, rhythmic throb rippled through her sex with each heartbeat. Still—

No. No, still, she wasn't going to let anything interfere with this. Well, anything besides her total lack of experience. She bit her lip and looked down at him. The long, thick length of his cock was sort of intimidating but she figured he'd fit well enough—that was the point of it, right? But getting to that stage was going to be tricky. Her face flushed and she slid him a nervous look.

"I don't really know what I'm doing, Blake," she whispered, blushing furiously.

His lids drooped low. In a hoarse voice, he said, "Lift up some."

She did and she stared, fascinated, as he wrapped his hand around his cock, pushing until the tip of it was pointing upwards instead of rigid against his belly. Her mouth went dry and she reached out, brushing the back of her knuckles down his length. In response to her touch, his cock jerked. Part of her wanted to explore this a little bit more, but a larger part was demanding she do this—*now*.

Now, before the need inside her killed her—and before she freaked out. "Just put your hand where mine is," Blake said. "Take your time. And if—"

"No ifs," she said, forcing a smile. She took him in her hand. He throbbed. His skin felt like silk stretched over the stiffened flesh of his cock. She held him steady and pressed against him. He trailed his fingers up her side, up her neck, brushed his fingertips over her mouth.

"I love watching you," he whispered, distracting her. He rested his other hand on her hip as she sank downward, slowly taking him inside. "You have no idea how many times I wished for this."

Del groaned at the feel of him inside her, stretching her, filling her. She fell forward, bracing her hands on his shoulders and wiggling a little as she tried to adjust "I can't believe I'm doing this," she said weakly, her voice hardly more than a faint squeak.

Her hair spilled down around them, her lids drooping low over her eyes and a feline smile curving her lips up. Her tongue slid out, tracing the upper curve of her lip. Blake didn't think he'd ever seen her look more beautiful.

He searched her face for some sign of fear but all he saw the beauty of a woman's pleasure. She squirmed again, wriggling her hips and trying to take him deeper. Catching her lip between her teeth, she said, "Help me out here."

Blake cupped her hips in his hands and held her steady, watching her face as he surged up. He watched for some flicker of pain, some flicker of fear. Her lids flickered and she winced, but then he was buried inside her, his cock swathed in sweet, satiny wet pussy. "Am I hurting you?" he demanded harshly.

"No," she whispered. Her voice shook and she made a sexy little humming sound deep in her throat, arching her back. That pose lifted her breasts and Blake groaned, pushing up onto his elbow so he could take one pink nipple into his mouth. Against her skin, he murmured again, "It's up to you, Del."

Slowly, she started to rock against him, tentative at first and awkward. He cupped her ass in his hands and fell back against the bed, watching her from under his lashes. Del found her pace soon enough and settled into a slow, lazy rhythm that set his blood to boiling.

His hands tightened and everything inside him cried for more. A lot more. Blake wanted to fist his hands in her hair and jerk her against him, roll over and put her beneath as he drove into her hard and fast. Instead, he gritted his teeth and fought to lay still. But he had to touch her. Laying his hand flat against her thigh, he slid it upward.

The curls covering her sex were pale, shades lighter

than her brown-dyed hair, soft buttery-yellow curls. Tight and hard, the bud of her clit lay hidden in those curls and Blake watched her face as he sought it out, watching her reaction. He circled it and smiled smugly as the tissues of her pussy clenched down around him.

Her thighs tightened around his hips and she shivered, her nails biting into his flesh. Del's lids fluttered low and then she opened her eyes, smiling down at him. "Do that again," she said, her voice husky.

"I will—if you lean down."

Del shifted forward again, resting her hands on the mattress by his head. Blake lifted up so he could taste her breasts again, first one, then the other. At the same time, he used his fingers on her, listening to her breathing and the soft broken moans to figure out what was the quickest way to make her moan, what made her shudder—what made her scream.

It was a sweet agony because every touch seemed to make her burn hotter, made her clench around him like a silken vise. She was so damn tight, virgin tight, and the wonder on her face as she started to come was the most beautiful, most erotic gift he'd ever been given—and the most amazing. His balls drew tight against him and fiery chills raced down his spine only seconds before he came, hard and fast. His hands clamped down on her hips and he arched up, circling his hips against hers. The slick, wet walls of her pussy gripped him tight convulsive caresses that milked him dry. Above him, Del screamed out his name and climaxed, her entire body tensing up and then slowly, a little at a time, she relaxed. From under his lashes, he watched as a faint, wondering smiled curved her lips and then she collapsed against him with a moan.

Blake slid his arms around her waist, breathing raggedly. "Are you okay?" he asked when he could finally speak.

"Um." Her voice was soft and drowsy. Blake craned his head around, staring at her face. A goofy, lopsided smile lit her face and she asked, "Define okay."

ഇ

It had been perfect. Del hadn't even let herself dream about something as sweet as that—so it only made sense that something would screw it up. She lay draped across his chest, nearly an hour after midnight, listening to his heart beat and just enjoying.

They'd made love twice.

Two whole times—and he'd made her come several times over. Each time. She could understand what in the hell had people so hot and bothered about sex. Logically, she'd already known that answer, but knowing it and *knowing* it were two different things. She knew, now, in every sweet, aching inch of her body, she knew.

He skimmed a hand up her side, cupped it over the back of her neck. Lifting his head, Blake brushed his lips against her temple and murmured softly, "You're so damn beautiful."

Just like that—Del was in hell.

The feel of his hand cupping the back of her head, his

words—it didn't matter that he felt nothing like her stepfather, that he looked nothing like her stepfather, that he smelled nothing like her stepfather. For a few heartbeats, she was trapped again, cruel hands pinioning both of hers together over her head while he crouched on top of her chest, shoving his dick inside her mouth. *That's it, Delilah. Look at you—you know you like this. You were made for it weren't you? You beautiful, perfect little slut. My little whore. Swallow it and tell me that you love it.*

When she sobbed instead, he'd hit her. Again and again, until she finally said what he wanted but her mouth was so swollen from his hitting her that he couldn't understand her.

Moaning under her breath, she jerked away from Blake and rolled off the bed, crouching beside it and rocking herself. Under her breath, she whimpered, unaware that she was whimpering and talking out loud. *Oh, God, oh, God, oh, God.*

At first, Blake hadn't understood what had happened. Drowsy, slipping closer and closer into true sleep, he had murmured to Del under his breath, stroking the soft silk of her hair and then—just like that, she was gone. Disoriented, he had pushed up onto his elbow just in time to see her disappear over the edge of the bed.

He couldn't see her, but the raw torment in her voice was like a knife in his heart, slowly twisting and destroying something inside him.

Damn you, Sanders, he thought, enraged. He climbed off the bed, but instead of going straight to Del, he paused long enough to pull something on. He couldn't find his pants so he settled on the black boxer briefs he'd worn earlier and hoped that would be enough for now.

Slowly, he went to her, feeling a little like he was approaching a wild animal—but this wasn't some unknown, abused puppy. This was Del—and that made it so much worse. It was Del, her eyes dark, glassy and terrified, staring sightlessly into the distance. He couldn't imagine what she saw, some hell that he couldn't even begin to imagine.

"Del?"

At first, she didn't even look at him. Then, stiffly, like it hurt to move, she turned her head, her gaze tracking him blindly and he knew she still wasn't aware of him. Keeping a good two feet between them, Blake crouched down in front of her. "Del, are you okay?"

She didn't answer. All Del did was lower her face and hide it against her knees. Her entire body trembled. Blake wanted to pull her against him and cuddle her—knowing that she probably didn't want him touching her, knowing she wouldn't welcome his comforting made the crack in his heart widen. Bitter helpless anger spilled out. "God, Del. Whatever I did, I'm sorry."

Seconds stretched out and when she finally responded, her words didn't make sense at first. "It wasn't what you did." Her shoulders lifted and fell as she heaved out a harsh breath. Eventually, she lifted her gaze and when she looked at him, it was with dry, bleak eyes. "It wasn't you, Blake."

Shaking his head, he whispered, "I can't believe that, Del. You were fine—" His hands closed into fists and it took a concentrated effort to make them relax. The last thing she needed from him was his anger. It wouldn't help her. And all it did to him was burn uselessly in his gut.

Her voice was soft as she began to speak, pulling his attention back to her. "A few years ago, there was this runaway I was trying to help. He'd come from a decent home, parents both worked, took care of him and his kid sister. Then they divorced, Mom got remarried, got pregnant...he decided to take off. Took a while to convince him that he needed to try to go back home, but I managed. Promised I'd come visit every now and then." A faint smile curled her lips. "He graduated three years ago and they invited me to this barbecue they were having for him. One of my first success stories. Anyway, when I went out there to see him, I saw his stepdad on the porch with this boy's little sister. She was eight. Had these big brown eyes and the sweetest smile. I watched them as they sat on the porch swing and laughed at a book. He picked her up and held her in a hug. It was one of the sweetest things I'd seen in a long time—and it put me back. I had to turn around and leave before they saw me. I barely made it to my car before I had a panic attack. I wasn't able to go to a silly barbecue all because I saw a guy hug his stepdaughter."

Her lids closed and she swallowed. Then she looked back at him and smiled. It was a wobbly smile and the sight of it dug new wounds into his heart. "They didn't cause it, but seeing them together brought it on. Doesn't make it their fault, any more than this is yours." Heaving out a sigh, she pushed her hair back from her face and then she stopped, frowned as she stared at her loose, dark hair.

She was looking at her hair. In a far off voice, Del said, "He used to grab me by my hair. The first thing I did when I made up my mind to leave was to cut it. I didn't do that consciously and I don't really even remember doing it. But I remember feeling it on my shoulders, my back and hating it. So I cut it all off. Took years to get the nerve to let it grow out a little."

The ends of her hair were just long enough to curl around her breasts. Hating the vivid pictures that her words painted, Blake tried to remember if he'd grabbed her hair. Had he? Shit. He stared at his hands, trying to remember—and failing.

"Blake."

Tearing his eyes away from his hands, he looked up at her.

She rolled to her knees, just a few inches away. Her hands came out and closed over one of his. "You didn't do this to me." Restlessly, she shrugged "But it happens. I come with baggage. A lot of it."

"I can deal with the baggage," Blake said, his voice tight and rusty. Felt like he was trying to force broken glass through his throat, not words. "What I can't deal with is not knowing what caused this."

A bitter smile curled her lips. "You really want to know? You called me beautiful."

Blake blinked. Yeah. He remembered that. He'd been drifting off, toying with her hair.

She twined her fingers with his, staring at their joined hands. "He used to call me his beautiful little whore. Said I was the perfect slut and everything he did to me, it was because that's what I was made for."

Blake snarled. He couldn't stop it. Surging to his feet, he started to pace the room. *Going to kill him,* Blake thought decisively. Didn't matter if he was caught or not because that sick monster just had to die.

Wide eyed, Del watched as Blake stormed up and down the gleaming wooden floor. His eyes were practically glowing red, he was so pissed off. He kept opening and closing his hands into fists and the violent anger inside him seemed to shimmer in the air around him.

But she wasn't afraid. It was strange. In that moment, she'd never seen a man more likely to do violence than Blake. He didn't just looked pissed. No, he looked like he was ready to peel away flesh, crush bone and pulverize body tissue. Yet Del wasn't afraid of him.

Now that she thought of it, though, she hadn't really been afraid of Blake, not even once. There'd been a couple of moments of knee jerk panic, but she didn't think she could say she it was a fear of *him.*

Even when he'd kissed her in the garage, it hadn't really been Blake that had set her off.

No.

That first kiss had been all of two days ago. Just two days. It was so hard to believe. It seemed like a lifetime since she'd driven back into Prescott, but it had only been three days. Technically, four. She figured it was past midnight on Sunday morning.

Fear was a part of her now and it had been for twelve years. Fear of men, in general and when she caught sight of a man who just vaguely resembled her stepfather, the knee jerk reaction was painful on a visceral level.

But not with Blake.

And, despite how much William Sanders repulsed her, despite the starring role he'd had in her nightmares, she didn't want Blake going after him.

Her skin felt cold, a little clammy as she pushed herself to her knees. Those memory flashbacks always did that.

She wanted a shower. Desperately. And she wanted Blake's arms around her while she had that shower. "Blake."

It took three tries before he finally heard her and by that point, he was going through the tall oak dresser in the corner of the room. Over his shoulder, their eyes met. "Don't, Blake."

A muscle in his jaw ticked as he stared at her. "Don't," she repeated. "This has already done me enough damage, and what you're thinking could land you in the county jail." Or the state penitentiary, but she didn't point that out. "I don't need to see that. *We* don't need it."

He looked away from her and she watched as he leaned against the dresser, bracing his hands against it. The muscles in his arms and back rippled. He dipped his head, staring at his feet. "I have to do something, Del. I have to make this better somehow."

"Blake." She waited until he looked at her and then she held out her hand. "Take a shower with me. Hold me. That is what's going to make this better."

He turned around and she watched as he twisted a T-shirt around his hands, bunching the fabric together and squeezing so tight, his knuckles went white. Slowly, he shook his head. "That's not enough."

Del cocked a brow. "It is for me. You want to make this better for me? Or for you, Blake?" She crossed over to him and gently pulled the shirt away from him, dropping it to the floor. Then she pushed up onto her toes and pressed her lips to the rigid line of his jaw. "I don't need some macho, possessive display of testosterone, Blake. I just need you right now."

Chapter Eight

I just need you.

You want to make this better for me? Or for you, Blake?

In retrospect, Blake had to admire Del's cleverness. There'd been no way he could say no to that. Even though he still wanted to feel Sanders's neck under his hands, every time he finally decided he was going to go and kill the bastard, he'd heard Del's voice again.

This has already done me enough damage, and what you're thinking could land you in the county jail.

He'd made himself a promise that he wasn't going to add damage, but he hadn't realized how hard it was going to be, keeping that promise.

His stomach rumbled demandingly but Blake ignored it, trying to focus on the report in front of him, instead of what had happened between him and Del Saturday night, stretching out in Sunday morning. They'd taken the pontoon out and found a secluded cove where he'd tried to convince her to skinny dip with him.

He'd made love to her again and while she slept in his arms out on the lake, he'd plotted, again, some painful way he could kill Sanders and not get caught. The lake itself was a temptation. Lake Cumberland was one big ass lake and there were lots of deep places. Someplace where a body could be put in a car and it might never be found.

Wasn't as painful as he'd like.

And unfortunately, Blake wasn't going to risk getting caught over it. He'd happily go to jail for the rest of his life if he could kill the bastard, but he was pretty sure Del wouldn't be pleased.

This has already done me enough damage.

At ten-oh-two on Monday morning, those words were still echoing in his mind and he couldn't, for the life of him, focus on the job. He'd been staring at the report detailing Junior's accident for a good twenty minutes and he couldn't have said for certain just what was on the piece of paper.

He heard a creak and glanced up to see Sam Beaumont standing in the doorway.

Blake leaned back in his chair and beckoned for Sam to come in. "I'm afraid I don't really have anything I can tell you right now..." His voice trailed off as he took in what Sam was wearing.

For Sam, it was practically formal attire. At least it was these days. Instead of his usual, torn, tight and faded jeans, he had on a looser pair, topped with a black polo. Both were clean, both were mostly free of wrinkles and he'd secured his long hair back from his face. Blake smiled and asked, "So did you dress up just to come see me, Sam?"

"Fuck off," Sam said affably as he dropped his long, lanky body into the rigid chair in front of Blake's desk. In his hand he held a file. Tapping it on his leg, he stared at Blake with unreadable, brown eyes. "Heard you left your reunion with Deedee. You two hooked back up already?"

Blake figured that had been about the twentieth time he'd heard that question in some form or another. And he gave Sam the same answer. "She's only been back here since Thursday. A little soon to tell."

Unfazed by the vague answer, Sam said, "Heard she'd settled in Cincinnati from Manda—saw Manda at the hospital this morning. She'd gone to say hi to Dad. You got any idea if Del's heading back home soon?"

Blake shrugged. He'd asked her that same question last night when he took her back to Manda's. He'd wanted to take her home with him, but he didn't want her to think he was trying to crowd her. Of course, that was exactly what Blake wanted to do, crowd her, keep her close by his side for the rest of their natural lives and never let a damn thing hurt her again. Brooding, he almost forgot that Sam was there and had just asked a question. "She took a few days off. Hanging around for a little while. Not sure how long."

"Hmmm." Sam looked back at the file he had in his hand. "You know...her dad was good friends with mine." He glanced up at Blake again, and there was an odd look in his piercing eyes. Blake waited him out but all Sam said was, "I'm going to be in the office, helping out with some things while Dad's recuperating."

"I see. And that's your professional attire?" Blake asked, tongue in cheek.

Sam laughed. "Yeah. This is pretty much it. Mom was almost over the moon when I told Dad I'd help him out for a while." In a slow, almost lazy move, he shoved to his feet and reached for the door. Pausing there, he glanced back at Blake. "Delilah was supposed to set up an appointment with Dad. Don't suppose you could tell her to call me about setting it up?"

Blake cocked a brow. "Don't know if she's going to be in town that long, Sam." He'd like to think she'd be around, but Blake wasn't counting on anything at this point.

Sam shook his head. "Not with Dad. With me. Got some business to discuss with her."

"Business?" Blake shook his head and asked, "What kind of..." His voice trailed off as he glanced back down at the file Sam held. He couldn't make out the name, but maybe Sam had already told him. More or less. Slowly, he nodded. "I'll pass the message on. We're meeting for lunch."

∞

"She called. Again." Manda glanced up from the stove as Del came in, heavy eyed, thirsty and starving. It had been midnight before she fell asleep, preoccupied with thoughts of Blake—who else? Dreams, interspersed with the odd nightmare, had tormented her for hours. Finally, sometime before dawn, she'd fallen into a more restful sleep.

At first, it took her a minute to figure out who, but the irritated look on Manda's face clued her in. "You wishing I'd rented a hotel room yet?"

Manda snorted. "Hell, no." A mean smile appeared on her face and she said, "Believe me, I'll tell that bitch you're unavailable until Doomsday and happily."

"Don't worry. You won't have to do it for too long." Del snagged a chair and pulled it out, collapsing into it so she could rest her head in her hands.

"Oh, don't tell me you're heading back already."

Del shook her head. "No. Actually, I should have told you before but I put in for some time off. Got a lot of time coming to me and I need a few more days anyway. But I don't want to wear out my welcome. Blake said that Bess still boarded the room over her store out. I was going to check that out."

"You will not." Manda turned around and glared at Del. "You'll damn well stay here."

"Manda—"

Her friend's eyes narrowed. "Don't argue with me. Geez, we got the room and I love the company." She made a face at the baby laying on the floor by the table. Avery was busy trying to fit her foot into her mouth and totally unaware of the adults grinning her way. "Believe me, I welcome to chance to actually talk with somebody who actually speaks back."

"Are you sure?"

Manda rolled her eyes. "Yes. I'm sure. But if it makes you feel any better..." She wagged her eyebrows. "You can baby-sit for me tonight. I'd love a night out with my husband."

"Baby-sit?" Del repeated, a little doubtful. Slowly, she looked back at the baby.

With an impish grin, Manda said, "Don't worry. You'll do fine."

∽

"Baby-sit?" Blake repeated. He laughed at the terrified look on Del's face and unable to resist, he leaned in and kissed her. "Don't look so worried. I don't think Avery's old enough for teeth so it's not like she can bite you."

She reached out and grabbed his hand, holding onto him like she was drowning. "You'll come by, help me out, right?"

"Sure." Blake pinched her chin and leaned back into the booth. "I'll even change a diaper or two."

Del, looking doubtful, asked, "You can change diapers?"

"I'm the uncle of three, I'll have you know. I've changed quite a few diapers." And he wouldn't admit, under threat of torture, how much it had terrified him those first few times. Instead, he gave Del an easy smile. "It's not that hard. Promise."

"Uh-huh." She settled back against the booth and wrapped her arms around her middle, still looking worried. "So how is Junior?"

"Doing fine. Out of ICU and he'll probably go home at the end of the week. Going to be a few more weeks recuperating at home, though." Remembering Sam's strange visit, he said, "By the way, you need to go see Sam Beaumont. He's helping out for a while. Senior is on his way back from Hawaii, took until this morning to get a flight back and he only works part time as it is. Anyway, Sam wants you to come by the office. Said you were supposed to see Junior over something...?"

"Yeah." Del propped her elbows on the table, a frown on her face. "I wasn't even here a day when Junior started trying to get a hold of me."

Darlene, the teenage waitress appeared to clear the table, and they fell quiet as she removed the plates.

"So what's he need to see you about?"

Del shrugged. "Not really sure. Guess I can walk by there now."

Stretching as he stood, Blake held out a hand. "I'll walk you." They left the café and headed down Main Street, hands linked. "So what time do I get to come over and make out with you while the baby sleeps?"

"Not making out allowed while I'm on duty," Del said, bumping her shoulder into his arm.

"You're no fun. Can I at least swipe a beer from the fridge?"

From the corner of his eye, he saw the smile on her

lips and he stopped walking, tugging her to a stop. Reaching up, he touched his finger to her mouth. "What's this for?"

She shrugged and blushed. "I don't know. Just kind of hard to believe I'm actually here with you." Like she was nervous, she averted her eyes for a minute and when she looked back at him, the look there just about drained the strength from his legs. "You wouldn't believe how often I thought about you."

Hooking his free arm around her neck, Blake replied, "Sure I would. Probably about as often as I thought of you." He kissed her, soft and slow, not lifting his head until she was breathing hard and arching against him. It was either stop then or find someplace private, real quick.

Somebody drove by and whistled and Blake glanced by with a grin. The police car disappeared around the corner and he rolled his eyes. "Come on before that idiot goes and spreads the word we're making out in the Square."

"Not like we haven't done that before," Del said, grinning. They fell back into step and another minute passed before she looked back at him. "So if we hadn't had a few roadblocks tossed at us, you think we'd be married and trying to con a friend into babysitting for us just so we can sneak a meal in peace?"

"Hey, no reason we can't still do that." He kept his voice casual as he came to a stop in front of the law office.

Her grin faded, replaced by a wistful expression. "Blake..."

Shaking his head, he said, "I'm not going to try to rush something on you, but I already told you that I never got over you. I don't see it happening either, not after twelve years of loving you."

She looked down and when her gaze came back up, her green eyes gleamed with tears. "Blake..." Her voice was thick and husky.

"Shhhh." He dipped his head and kissed her softly. "Don't go thinking about it too much if you're not ready for it. But I did figure I should probably let you know that I still love you."

Then he tugged his hand away, gesturing towards the door as it opened to reveal Sam standing there. Slowly, she backed away and turned. Blake watched as she climbed exactly two steps and then stopped and turned back around. She jumped down the steps and reached for him, wrapping her arms tight around his neck.

Her hurried whisper was faint, but Blake heard it as clearly as if she had screamed it from the Square. *I love you, too.*

He was still grinning as she ran back up the steps and disappeared inside with Sam.

∞

"You look a bit different from the last time I saw you," Sam said as he led her toward the large office in the back. It was his father's, but he seemed as comfortable in it as if it was his name on the diplomas and certificates hanging on the walls in black frames.

Del skimmed a look over Sam Beaumont and grinned. "Gotta say, the same goes for you." The last time she could remember seeing him had been the summer she was fifteen. He'd come home from college and he'd looked exactly like what he had been—a bored rich kid killing time at home over summer break. She'd heard enough stories about him. Even though she was over-the-moon crazy for Blake, Sam had been good looking enough, with a slightly dangerous edge, that even she hadn't been totally blind to him.

That slightly dangerous edge had been replaced. Once, that danger had been just a possibility. Now, Sam seemed to exude an aura of menace. He settled down behind a large mahogany desk and she studied his face as she took the chair directly in front of him. His face had matured but the planes and angles were all the same, his craggy good looks just a little bit rougher.

His eyes had changed the most. They weren't the same at all. They were harder. Colder. Flatter.

Del had seen a similar look in her own eyes a time or two and she wondered what had happened to him, who he'd lost. But she wasn't here for some kind of personal discussion with Sam. She just wanted to see why his father, and now Sam, kept pestering her.

"So why am I here, Sam?" she asked, leaning back into the soft, plush leather.

He crooked a brow at her. He had his dad's dark brown eyes and like his dad, he could show as much or as little emotion as he chose. The longish hair and his casual clothes didn't detract from the comfortable way he flipped through the file on the desk in front of him, pausing to study one sheet. "Been going through some information and it looks like my father left a number of messages with your mother, sent her correspondence a half dozen times over the past few years."

With a shrug, Del said, "I don't know why that affects me. Mom and I aren't really on speaking terms."

Sam nodded, still studying the file. He reached up, idly stroked his chin. "How long has it been since you talked with her, f you don't mind my asking?"

"Twelve years."

That caught his attention. He looked up from whatever he'd been reading. He blinked and then glanced back down at the file frowning. With a flick of his wrist, he closed the file and leaned back into his chair, watching her closely. "Twelve years."

Del nodded. "I haven't seen her or talked to her since I was sixteen, Sam."

"Hmmm." With a long-fingered hand, Sam reached up and rubbed the back of his neck. "She never sent you any letters at school? Never came to visit?"

"I didn't go to school, Sam," Del replied, her voice flat. Although Del knew the highlights, she didn't know the specifics of whatever fantasy world Louisa had painted to explain Del's absence and in all honesty, she cared very little. Way too little to even consider going along with whatever stories her mother had told.

"Twelve years," Sam whispered.

He looked up at her again and this time, when their gazes met, she saw that his was cold and hard. He glanced at the clock hanging on the wall and then back at her. "This is going to take a while. Have you got the time?"

Del, getting irritated, demanded, "What is going to take a while?"

Slowly, Sam looked down and flipped the file in front of him back open. He pulled out a rather legal looking document and then he turned it around so that she could read the ornate script across the top of it.

"Your father's will, Del. And a trust fund that you should have inherited when you turned twenty-one."

Mouth dry, Del parroted back, "Trust fund?"

Sam's mouth quirked in a grin. "Enough that you wouldn't ever have to work again." His grin faded. "There was also a large sum set aside for your college education and I do mean, *large*. It would have paid for a four-year education at just about any Ivy League school in the country, as well any other schooling you might have needed. Law school, medical school—it would have paid for Harvard, Yale, Princeton. Anywhere."

Yale. Back before Daddy had died, she used to tell him she wanted to be a doctor. She could remember him smiling down at her and telling her she could do anything, be anything she wanted. Yale—she'd busted her ass just to get through a state-funded community college, living in low-income housing and damn near killing herself to keep her grades high enough that she wouldn't lose the grants and scholarships that Joely had helped her get and there had been money for her to go to Yale.

Looking up, Del met his eyes. "I don't know anything about it." Her head pounded furiously as she tried to wrap her mind around what Sam had just told her. Good grief, how many times had she skipped eating dinner so she'd have enough money to pay rent, pay tuition once she started college? She wouldn't let herself think about the years when she'd been too high to care that she was sleeping in the streets. Money, at that point, wouldn't have helped and it probably would have made it worse. Made the drugs she craved that much more accessible.

But after? Damn, when she'd gotten herself straightened out there had been times when she'd been so hard up for money, she'd sold plasma just to buy Ramen noodles. Times when she had worked forty hours a week flipping burgers and going to school full time. There had been many, many nights when Del had gotten less than four hours of sleep. "I had no idea."

Sam shrugged. "Considering you left home before you could access it, even with the trustee's permission, that's not a surprise. No, what is kind of surprising is the fact that Dad has done nearly everything he could think of to get you to the office. Sent registered letters to your mother's house and she told him, repeatedly, that the letters were all forwarded onto you but she wouldn't ever give him that forwarding address. He took out notices in every major paper for the past five years, trying to find you. I know for a fact that he went by your mother's house quite often hoping to get some information on your whereabouts." With a faint smile, Sam said, "It was like you'd dropped off the earth. Of course, your mom's told people about you finishing school up over in Europe. Spent some time in France."

Her eyes burned as she looked at Sam. "I never went to France, Sam. I never graduated high school. I got my GED when I was 19."

If he was surprised, it never showed. One black brow went up slightly and he nodded. "Dad's the trusting sort. Your mother tells him that you're living the high life in New York, Los Angeles and Chicago, he takes her at her word. He took out ads in easily a half dozen major newspapers hoping you'd see them but that's about as far as he went" Sam gave her a sardonic grin. "Me, I don't trust people any further than I can throw them so I called a friend who used to help me out when I was working in Nashville."

He held her gaze as he withdrew a piece of paper from the file on the desk and laid it down in front of her. Del kept her hands clenched in her lap and hoped they weren't shaking as she skimmed the list. It pretty much detailed her life from the time she'd been founding bleeding to death in the rest stop ten years earlier.

"Any reason you're so damn curious about my life, Sam?" she asked, forcing the words out through a throat as dry and rough as sandpaper.

"Delilah."

His voice was gentle, a lot more gentle than she would have expected coming from somebody like Sam. Slowly, she looked up at him and found him staring at her with compassionate eyes. "I don't know what happened that made you run away from home, and I don't need to know. But I know when a woman's been through hell. I've seen it, all too often. Whatever has happened in your past belongs to you, and you alone. But I needed to know why Dad wasn't ever able to find you. You're the heir to an estate that is valued in the millions. And..." His voice trailed off and he looked down, as though trying to figure out how to say something that wasn't going to be much fun. Not for him to say and not for her to hear.

"Spit it out, Sam," Del said, her voice harsh. This wasn't his fault, logically she knew that and she could even understand why he'd paid somebody to root around in her life. But she was still humiliated. Still furious. Sick inside.

"Delilah, your father left you damn near everything. Including the house. When you turned twenty-one, it was to revert to you."

"Everything?" she repeated.

"With the exception of a monthly stipend for your mother, and a lump sum that she would have received when you turned twenty-one, yes."

Most of what Sam went on to explain was a lot more legal-eze than Del could follow, but after he explained the legal crap, he laid it out in plain and simple English. There was a lot more than just the house and the trust fund. A lot.

Del had been eight when her dad died. Too young to

understand or even know about all the legal ramifications that came along with death. Twenty years had passed since her father died and every month since then, her mother had been issued a check that was meant for Delilah.

"The money from a trust can be used in a variety of ways. Clothing, food, childcare—any of these. You were a minor and so your mother was in charge of the money." His voice seemed to drone on and from time to time, he'd look up at her, as if to make sure she was still following him.

Desperate to get out of there, to get some place quiet, some place alone, and just *think*, Del nodded as though he made perfect sense. Truth be told, she'd stopped really processing his words a while back.

Money. Money for food. Money for school.

Del hadn't ever needed for money growing up. She always had new clothes, very nice new clothes, plenty of cash to spend, she'd even gotten a new car for her sixteenth birthday.

There had been times after she'd run away from home when she barely recognized herself, living on the street, stealing food, stealing money to *buy* food. And drugs, she thought bitterly. Can't forget the drugs. She'd given years of her life to drugs and all that pain and misery had pushed her down the road to that rest stop where she'd tried to kill herself.

That had been the catalyst that turned her life around and she wasn't going to forget anything that led her to that point.

She was missing entire pieces of her life, pieces she'd never get back. During that bleak stretch of time, nearly three years in all, there had been days when she'd been too drunk or too high—or both, to know where she was or even care. Del had moved around a lot, even after she'd sobered up while she tried to figure out what to do with herself.

Del couldn't really fault her mother for not being able to find her and relay the message from the lawyer. But Louisa had been lying about it—for *years*. More than that, Louisa was apparently still cashing those monthly checks. Louisa let people think that Del was getting the money and out living the high life—finishing up high school in France and jet setting around Europe.

That was what made Del sick. She tried not to think about how many nights she had spent in some shelter, or how hard she'd busted her ass to put herself through college once she straightened out and got her GED.

As hard as those years had been, Del knew that if she could have traded her real history for the one her mother had fabricated for her, she wouldn't do it. The rapes? Yes, she would have undone that hell in a heartbeat, but what came after? No. All of that had led her to what she was now—the woman she was now was a hell of a lot stronger than the girl she had been. The woman she was now made a difference. She'd saved lives and some of that had come from her own experiences in hell.

Undoing those years would undo all of the things that

had happened since and she wouldn't do it. The life her mother described was meaningless.

The past had put her on the path she was on now and the fact that her mother had been lying and filling people's heads with some fake life of luxury made Del irrationally furious. Even madder than the fact that Louisa was living in the house that belonged to Del. Banking money that belonged to Del.

Hundreds of thousands of dollars—and there were *millions* in the bank, just waiting for a signature from Del to be all hers. Each time Junior had tried to contact Del, Louisa had made him believe she was relaying the messages to her daughter and that Del wasn't interested in coming home to see her to affairs, that she preferred Louisa to remain in charge.

She had a headache from clenching her jaw by the time it was all done. Sam called the secretary, Paulette, in to act as a witness while Del signed the necessary paperwork. Del gripped the fountain pen so hard, it wouldn't have surprised her if it broke and she signed her name in an angry scrawl before slamming the pen down.

After the sweet-faced, black woman had added her signature, Sam said, "Paulette, why don't you go ahead and take your lunch? You never did get one earlier—tell you what, why don't you turn the phones over and then you could go ahead and take off for the day. You could swing by the hospital and see Dad. Mom promised my sister she'd go into Lexington while Jenny had her ultrasound and Dad wouldn't let them reschedule so he hasn't had any company today. I bet he'd love to see you.

Especially if you snuck him some fried chicken from the diner."

Whatever the secretary said fell on unhearing ears as Del sat in the chair, her nails digging into the armrests and her gut in a knot. The door closed behind her and she didn't even move. It wasn't until Sam got up from the chair and headed towards her that she reacted. Already tense and on edge, her body perceived damn near everything as a threat right now and she shot up from the chair, moving so that the big leather piece was between her and the man watching her with calm, measuring eyes.

She saw the knowledge in his eyes and she flushed, furiously. He held up his hands in a calming gesture and instead of coming any closer, he settled lean hips on the edge of the desk. He tucked his hands into his pockets and looked like he was doing his damnedest to appear non-threatening. Not the easiest task for a man who looked like he did.

"I'll walk you over to the bank so you can talk to the manager. Most of this is just a formality because the money technically has been yours for seven years now."

Del nodded jerkily. Although she desperately wanted to be alone right now, she wanted this over with. But she didn't trust herself to speak rationally just yet, considering how mad she was getting. Madder than she had ever been, and it was getting worse by the second.

"If you like, when we're done, I can go with you to speak to the sheriff."

Sheriff. Her face blank, she looked at Sam and

repeated, "The sheriff?"

He inclined his head. "Delilah—"

"Del," she corrected. "Call me Del. Please."

He nodded. "Del, you do understand what your mother has done, don't you?"

She bared her teeth at him in a mockery of a smile. "Damn straight I do. My beloved mama has stolen money from me. A lot of money."

Sam shrugged. "That, I can't swear to and even though I suspect it, you need to know that there's a possibility nothing will happen. Particularly if she can account for the money. All she has to do is claim she was managing it for you until you came home." He flicked a glance at the half-buried report on the desk and added, "A smart lawyer could have her claim that she was aware of your...less than wise choices and that she was simply safeguarding your interests until she knew you could be trusted."

Finally, she figured out why he had suggested the sheriff's office. A mean smile curled her lips and she debated doing just that. She would just love to see a uniformed deputy and the county DA speaking with her mother in some small room with two-way glass, demanding to know why the woman had been helping herself to money that belonged to Del.

But...*no.*

She wouldn't do it. Deep inside, in some small part of her heart, she still loved her mother—or at least, she loved the *ideal* of her mother, a woman who loved her, a woman who cherished her—a woman who would protect her.

She could remember times when she'd been a child and her parents had come into her room at night time. Dad would read her a story while Mom brushed her hair. After Dad died, her mother had become more distant, but now Del realized that distance had always been there—it had just been buffered by the loving presence of her father.

It would damn well serve Louisa right if Del did try to press charges. And she knew it was still possible it could happen even if she chose not to pursue it on her own. She knew enough about the law to know that the DA may decide to investigate the matter. Hundreds of thousands of dollars, possibly even millions, that was supposed to go to Del had instead gone to Louisa. Each time the woman had signed one of those monthly checks and kept the money, she had committed a crime. Yes, Del had to be the one to sign the paperwork and take responsibility of her inheritance, but Louisa had deliberately set out to convince Junior that she was simply acting at her daughter's request.

Whether or not Louisa would be found guilty was meaningless, or at least it was to Del. It wasn't all that likely that Louisa would ever be found guilty anyway. The woman was too slick, too adept at manipulating people. She'd play a jury like a master violinist could play a violin.

Still, if the DA decided to press charges, Louisa would be humiliated—for that alone, Del was tempted.

If Del had been eaten up with the idea of getting justice, she probably would have happily pursued it—but she was more interested in *payback* than justice. The thought of her mother in jail, although it was a slim chance, wasn't one that settled well with Del. Having people see Louisa as she truly was...yeah, there was some appeal.

Too much appeal. She wanted to see that just a little too much, and not for the right reasons. Or at least, not *all* of them.

So she'd let it go.

But by damn, Del *was* taking her house. She might even take a wrecking ball to the wing where Mommy dear and that perverted bastard Sanders slept. And her room was going to be gutted—she might even be the one to hold the sledgehammer.

That was her house, damn it. Her dad had left it to her and she would rather shave her head bald than let Sanders live there another minute.

Her voice was flat and steady when she finally replied, "I'd appreciate you coming with me to the bank. But the sheriff's office isn't necessary." She smiled a little and said, "I know that this will be reported to the county DA and if he decides to press charges, so be it. I'll do what's necessary at that point. But on a personal level, I don't need it. However...I'd like it if you would come with me to the house tonight, if you can."

Sam glanced at his watch. "We could go now, if you'd like."

Del shook her head. "No. I want to take care of the business at the bank and then I need some time by myself. And I want Blake to come with me."

Sam's mouth canted up at one corner. "For legal support? Or personal?"

With a smile, Del replied, "Personal. You're the legal support."

Chapter Nine

She was sweating.

Louisa Prescott Sanders was sweating. With a surreptitious glance, she made sure the nursing staff was otherwise occupied. Twice monthly, Louisa volunteered at the small county hospital and she knew the middle of the afternoon was a chaotic time at the hospital. Shift changes, doctors making their rounds, family visiting, yes, it was sheer chaos.

Chaotic enough that few would take note of a flower delivery. Now that Beaumont Junior was out of intensive care, the flowers were a wonderful cover up. She had pulled her hair into a ponytail and wore a disgustingly grimy baseball cap to cover her carefully colored and highlighted hair. The baggy T-shirt and jeans disguised her figure and she wore large, oversized sunglasses. It wasn't, perhaps, the most clever disguise, but all she needed to do was avoid being noticed.

With any luck, Junior would be in a narcotic-induced slumber and he would never realize she'd been there. One tiny little prick, a few moments, and then this would be over.

There would, of course, have to be some sort of incident at his office. She imagined a fire would suffice and she already had a man in mind for that job. William did have a rather colorful, extensive network of people and with the right sum, she could buy the services she needed, and their silence.

She tucked a hand into the baggy pocket on her left hip and wrapped her hand around the syringe. Last week when she had heard Delilah was indeed back in town, she'd realized she might have to take drastic measures. The insulin had been in Marcy Baylor's refrigerator, left over from her pregnancy and after she'd delivered a rather large baby, the woman hadn't discarded the vial. Marcy's pregnancy-induced diabetes was now under control and it had given Louisa the perfect way to kill.

Nobody could track the medicine back to her and after she was done, she would dispose of the vial in a way that it couldn't possibly be found. She doubted Marcy would even remember that she had left the vial in her refrigerator. Quite perfect, all in all.

Louisa had intended to use the insulin on her daughter. Upon Delilah's death, everything reverted back to the last living relative and that was Louisa. But Junior had been too persistent, determined to get Delilah into the office to discuss the last will and testament of Louisa's late husband. Her lip curled in a sneer but it lasted only a second before she made the conscious effort to smooth her features. Every ugly emotion would show on the face in time and Louisa worked hard to maintain a flawless visage.

If Douglass hadn't been such a fool about his beloved Delilah, none of this would have been necessary. She had imagined that Douglass would see to it that Delilah was provided for, but to leave her nearly everything? As his wife, Louisa had been entitled to a third of his estate— perhaps, if Douglass had left her Prescott Manor and some of his other properties, Louisa might have been satisfied.

But the man hadn't done that, now had he?

It was his fault, his mistake, but it was up to Louisa to rectify it. She kept a watchful eye out as she eased open the door to Junior's room, but a familiar voice had her freezing in place.

"Now if I get caught serving you up this chicken, it's your boy's fault," Paulette said.

Louisa was too much of a lady to swear, but at that moment, several very colorful phrases danced through her mind. She heard footsteps and quickly, she lifted the huge vase of flowers, shielding her face. With one more glance around, she backed away from the door and then, spying the empty room next to Junior's, she slid inside. The door to the bathroom was open and she ducked inside, turning the lock and then setting the flowers on the sink so she could lean against the connecting door and listen.

Paulette had a voice as big as her body, deep and booming, and it carried. Junior's voice was stronger than it had been and as he spoke, it sent a fission of nerves coursing through Louisa. "So Sam was with Delilah as you left? The papers are all signed?"

"Finally," Paulette said, heaving out a loud sigh. "Bout time, too. I'm telling you, Junior, that mama of hers ought to be strung up, letting this carry on so long."

Junior chuckled while, hiding inside the bathroom, Louisa's face turned red. That nasty, insolent bitch, she thought. How dare she? Junior was too magnanimous by far, letting a paid employee speak like that about any client—but *especially* one of Louisa's background and breeding.

"Louisa just has her own way of doing things, Paulette. We know that. Although I must admit, I'm very glad that Sam took this mess into his hands before Delilah tried to slip away again. I'd already made up my mind if I didn't manage to speak with her while she's in town, I was going to hire a private investigator to track her down. I let this go on far too long."

"Well, it's done now. I saw them on my way out of the diner and they were going into the bank. Going to speak with Stu, I'd say," Paulette said. "I'll tell you, Junior, Delilah did not look happy. Not one bit."

Junior said something else, but Louisa was already backing away. She slid out of the room, her mind working furiously. She forgot about the flowers until she was at the stairs and at that point, she was too worried to go back for them.

It was too late to silence the Beaumonts now—either of them. She hadn't ever expected Sam to step into his father's shoes and that had been a foolish mistake on her part. She had been prepared to deal with Beaumont

Senior when he returned. Very little would have been necessary after she'd dealt with the law office. One couldn't read a will if it was all in ashes. Louisa had destroyed her copy in a fury of pique years earlier and she already had plans on how to get the one from the bank manager's office.

Stu Harding was her age and the man had always had his eye on her. She had plans to visit him the very next day, right at closing. She'd express some concern over something in the will—and with Junior being indisposed, naturally, she had thought of Stu. He would open the safe and while he was doing that, she'd pour them both some of the bourbon he kept there.

A few drinks, a little flattery—as well as some Xanax slipped into his drink and Louisa would be gone and Stu's copy of the will destroyed. It was a joy living in a small town. Stu wouldn't even remember her visit, she knew because the man had a poor head for drinking. He lost entire hours to the drink if he wasn't cautious and Louisa would see to it that Stu lost all caution.

All of her planning, though, and it was for naught.

She took the stairs at a fast clip, determined to get away before one soul recognized her. On her way out the door, she tucked a hand into her pocket and closed it around the syringe. It would have been easier to take care of Junior. In a hospital, people received the wrong medicine from time to time but it would be harder for people to see that happening to Del.

Still, all Louisa needed was a plan. Nobody would

believe she was capable of killing her own daughter. Louisa truly hated that it had come to this, although not because she had fond feelings for Delilah. The girl hadn't ever been the daughter that Louisa had imagined. More concerned about herself and her own needs than that of the family name and the responsibilities that came with it.

Delilah was such a waste and sadly, it was up to Louisa to deal with the mess.

It was all Douglass's fault that this was necessary.

∞

Her soft mouth set in a frown, Del glared at him and crossed her arms over her chest. Blake noted with some surprise that Del had painted her nails. It wasn't the pale cotton candy pink he remembered her wearing so often in school, rather an intense, crimson red. The strong, bold color suited the woman before him better than pink ever could.

"You don't look all that surprised," she said, her voice cool and flat.

With a shrug, Blake replied, "Honestly, I'm not. As long as she doesn't have to get her lily-white hands dirty, Louisa's capable of a lot of things." Leaning back in his chair, he studied the sheaf of papers she'd thrust into his hands the second she's stalked into his office.

He skimmed over the notes jotted down in Junior's sweeping scrawl, noting the dates and times that Junior had made attempts to speak with Louisa. Hundreds of messages left. Ideally, Blake figured the best thing Junior could have done was contact a private investigator to track Del down, like Sam had done. He grimaced as he thought of how Del's privacy had been invaded, but she shouldn't have spent the past twelve years struggling. There was enough money that she shouldn't have spent even five seconds worrying about money.

Juggling the figures in his head, he came up with some numbers. Assuming that until Del signed whatever papers were required, there was six thousand dollars a month coming out of the trust fund that should have been used for her needs, food, clothes, rent if she was so inclined, that was almost three quarters of a million dollars that should have been hers since she turned eighteen. The majority of her father's estate should have gone directly to her upon her twenty-first birthday, including the house, and still Louisa and William lived there, in Del's home, like royalty.

Money set aside for college that Del had never received. And all the money that had been set aside while Del was still a minor, money that should have been used for her and it was made out to Louisa. No, Del hadn't ever lacked for anything. Louisa was too caught up in her own self-importance to let her daughter go around dressed in clothes from Wal-Mart. But how much of that six thousand a month had actually gone to Del? Very little.

Millions of dollars, he figured. Louisa had been reaping the benefits of Del's inheritance, probably ever since Douglass Prescott had died, and she would have gone on doing just that if Del hadn't come home. Louisa was accustomed to a certain life and he knew she loved her money, but Douglass's will had set aside a decent monthly sum for his wife upon his death. Why had she worked so hard to keep Del from getting what was rightfully hers?

"So will you?"

Blake glanced up and swore softly. "I'm sorry, baby. I was thinking about something."

Del rolled her eyes. "I need to go out to the manor tonight. I want you to come with me. I was asking if you would."

Oh, there was no way in hell he would let her go out there alone. "Absolutely." With a wicked grin, he asked, "You want me to bring a few deputies and you can watch while we make them vacate the premises?"

She laughed and he felt his heart clench at the sound. "No. But I do want a witness when I tell her she has thirty days to find some place else to live."

"You're too nice," Blake said, shaking his head. "I'd kick them out tonight." Pensively, he studied her face. "Sanders will be there."

As though she was chilled, Del rubbed her arms with her hands. "Yeah, I know." She shrugged, but the movement looked oddly mechanical and he knew she was nowhere near as calm as she wanted to be. "Got to face him sooner or later—and telling him to get out of my house sort of sounds like fun."

"Fun." Blake grinned and shook his head. "No, sugar. Fun would be letting me pound him into a pulp. *That* would be fun."

Then he cocked a brow at her. "Hey, I can think of something else that's fun."

The grim look in Del's eyes faded, exactly as he'd hoped, and she smiled at him. "Knowing your mind, I can only guess."

"You know me so well." Glancing at the door behind her, he said, "Why don't you turn that lock?"

Del slid him a narrow glance but then reached behind her and locked the door. Then she hooked her thumbs in the pockets of her jeans and gave him a teasing smile. "Why am I locking the door, Blake?"

Instead of answering her, he crooked a finger at her.

Del sauntered around the desk, coming to a stop just beside him and leaning a hip against the edge. "You know, I have a feeling that whatever you're planning could get the two of us in trouble."

Spinning around his chair, he reached out and grasped her hips, tugging her close. Through the thin cotton of her shirt, he could feel the warmth of her skin, could smell the soft, female scent of her. "Hmmm. Maybe. But I don't plan on telling anybody. Do you?"

She brought up a hand, curved it over the back of his neck. "Oh, I dunno. Blackmail material could always come in handy, especially with you law enforcement types." She smiled at him but when he cupped a hand between her thighs, rubbed the heel of his palm against her sex, she blushed and sent a worried look towards the door.

"Blackmail material, huh?" He turned her around, tugged her down until she was sitting on his lap. "Well, considering the way you scream..."

It didn't seem possible, but she blushed even harder, red all the way to the roots of her hair. Squirming against his hands, she mumbled, "You're awful, Blake."

"Hmmmm. And you're sweet," He trailed his fingers up her thigh, over her hip until he could stroke the bare skin of her belly under the waistband of her shirt. When he slid the button of her pants free, he paused, gave her a minute to refuse, but she didn't breathe a word. "Real sweet. And hot..." He pushed his hand inside her jeans, inside her panties and then dipped two fingers, quick and light, inside her pussy. "And *wet*...Damn it, Del."

She whimpered and rocked her hips upward against his hand.

"Shhh," he murmured into her ear. "Otherwise you and me really might get in trouble here." He circled a thumb around her clit. "I want to make you come, right here, right now. You think you can do it without screaming?"

Del swallowed and looked once more towards the door.

Blake nuzzled her neck. "Nobody can come in. The door's locked, remember? And as long as you don't scream..." As he spoke, he screwed two fingers in and out of her sex and when her lips parted, he used his free hand to angle her face around and he caught her mouth with his own.

"Don't scream," he warned against her lips.

"Blake, please..." She rocked against his hand, worked her hips in a desperate circle.

He continued to stroke her, toying with her until she was whimpering and pleading in a low, hoarse whisper. "You have no idea what it does to me, seeing you like this," he rasped, lifting his head and staring down at them. His hand lost to sight inside Del's pants, her chest rising and falling with harsh, ragged breaths. Through the layers of her shirt and bra, he could see the hard, pebbled crests of her nipples. Her head rested against his shoulder, her cheeks flushed, her lashes low over her eyes. She was so damn beautiful, it hurt to even look at her. All he wanted to do was tell her that, but memories of what had happened over the weekend still loomed like in an ugly shadow in his mind.

So instead of telling her that, he feathered a kiss across her cheek and whispered, "Kiss me, Del."

She turned her face to his and when their lips met, he circled his thumb once more around her clit and started to pump his fingers in and out of her sex in a quick, steady rhythm.

It didn't last long enough. Del responded to his touch like she'd been created just for him, made to react like this, only for him. When she came, she cried out, but he muffled the sound of it with his lips.

After it was over, he adjusted her clothes and then wrapped his arms around her waist, holding her as her breathing slowed. "You did that on purpose," she said a few minutes later, her voice soft and drowsy.

"Damn straight. I don't know how I could get you to come on accident,"

Del snorted. "Smart ass," she mumbled. Then she pushed lightly against his hands, straightening up so that she sat on his lap instead of sprawling back against him. "I meant you did that to distract me."

"Guilty."

Turning her head, she pressed her lips to his cheek. "Thank you."

Blake laughed, cupped her hips in his hands, holding her as he nudged his swollen cock against her butt. "Oh, don't thank me now." He wagged his brows at her. "Thank me later."

℘

"This is insane."

William Sanders listened as his wife spoke about killing her daughter the same way she'd speak about having a new room added on to the house. Calm and matter of factly, as though it meant less than nothing.

"William, we simply have no choice."

He shoved a hand through his thinning hair and turned away. "The hell we don't."

From her chair by the window, she sipped her coffee and then leveled her pale green eyes on his face. "And what other choice do we have?"

William waved a hand. "It's her inheritance that you've been spending. We'll just pay her back."

"And the house?"

He glanced around the opulent solarium and then back at his wife. "If it's her house, she can have it."

"Do you really think that she will be satisfied with that?" Louisa asked. Setting aside her coffee cup, she rose and smoothed down her skirt. It fell to her knees without a wrinkle, without a crease. "She hasn't forgotten what you did to her, William. She will want to make us suffer for it."

Wary, he eyed her as she moved closer. "I didn't do anything to her, Louisa. She was a troubled child and she—"

In a calm voice, with a pleasant smile, Louisa said, "I know what happens in my house, William. Exactly."

Fear wrapped a fist around his heart as she met his gaze. He saw the knowledge in her eyes and his mouth went dry as he realized what this could mean for him.

She reached out and patted his cheek gently. "Don't look so frightened, William. I know what happens in my house but that doesn't mean that I wish for everyone to know. If you had kept your indiscretions away from here, it would have been better but this is nothing that we cannot deal with. But we must handle Delilah before she ruins the both of us."

With a shake of his head, he said, "We can't expect to kill her and nobody look at us for it. We'd inherit everything. That will automatically make us suspects."

Louisa smiled. "Now. Just leave that to me."

William almost argued with her. Then he thought better of it. Whatever Louisa had planned, it was best that he knew nothing. If she actually did try to kill Delilah— worse, if she succeeded, then he wanted to be able to say he knew nothing about it.

℣℥

"Idiot." Louisa left William alone in the solarium a few minutes later. She had poured him a drink and stayed long enough to make sure he drank it then she had carried the brandy snifter into the kitchen and washed it herself. It wouldn't do for the police to find the glass. Surely the Xanax that she'd ground up would leave some sort of residue.

On her way back to her personal office, she'd paused by the solarium and smiled with satisfaction as she watched William dozing off on the sofa. She did like that sofa. It would be a shame that she'd have to discard it. Sometime soon, she expected it would be liberally splattered with blood.

The solution to her problem had come to her on the way home and she'd known what she had to do.

If she knew her stubborn daughter, then Delilah would be at the house sometime tonight. Delilah's own sordid past was going to provide the perfect cover up. Several suicide attempts, the drugs, even Delilah's bizarre appearance, all of it would simply add more credence to the story the cops would hear.

As repellent as it was, even the meeting between Sam and Delilah would work in Louisa's favor. Louisa already planned to explain that she'd kept the money from her daughter out of motherly concern—after all, a drug addict couldn't be trusted with millions. Nobody would fault her, once they knew the truth about Delilah's shadowy past.

And it gave Delilah a motive for murder without Louisa having to share tawdry, tasteless information with public servants.

William was already dealt with—between the Xanax and the brandy, William would be sound asleep when she killed him. He'd never even know what hit him.

It wouldn't be long before Delilah was as well.

Louisa had already rehearsed what she'd say...*I came in when I heard the noise. William was taking a nap. He'd been so upset lately...*A few tears, a wobble in her voice, and then she'd sigh, and force herself to continue. *I grabbed the gun from William's office and ran to see what had happened. I saw Del standing over him with a gun. She shot him, and then she pointed the gun at me. I thought she'd shoot me...I screamed, and I...Oh, my God. I shot my daughter. I just...I was so terrified...*

Louisa ran through the plan in her mind once more. When Del arrived, Louisa would lead her into the living room—then she'd shoot William. Perhaps a few tears, on Louisa's part, a few false sobs. *He told me, darling. He told me what he'd done to you, and I simply had to do it. I wanted you to see how sorry I was...*She'd get Delilah into the living room, close to William, and then Louisa would shoot the selfish bitch.

Louisa had dismissed the staff shortly after coming home. She had tearfully explained to Trish, their housekeeper, that she needed some time alone. *Delilah still refuses to come visit. Whatever did I do to make her hate me so?* Trish was everything that Louisa required of an employee, prompt, honest, hardworking and discreet. She knew when to speak and when not to. When the police questioned Trish, she would share with them how distraught Louisa had been since her only child had come back home but refused any contact with her family.

She's a troubled girl, Sheriff. Since she left, she's had problems with drinking, with drugs. I just never imagined she'd do a thing like this. Louisa was glad she'd kept tabs on Delilah, now more than ever. The private investigator had been hired out of Louisville and paid cash and it was one of the best investments she had made. She knew Delilah's history of alcohol abuse, her drug abuse. It would all work very well for Louisa.

With her right hand gloved and the gun ready, she sat down at her desk and watched outside. Waiting to see Delilah's beat-up car come around the corner.

"Some things never do change, Delilah." Delilah had Douglass's sense of justice and this one time, it was going to help Louisa instead of irritate her.

Hearing the car, she stood up from her desk and hurried downstairs. A quick glance into the solarium assured her that William was still asleep. The car stopped and she listened for the knock, keeping her gloved hand tucked behind her back. The gun was growing heavier and although she wouldn't dare to admit it, she was sweating from nerves.

As she rounded the corner, she forced herself to smile so she'd be ready when she greeted Delilah. But there was no knock.

Instead, she heard the snick of a lock and she stopped in the hallway as the door opened. The smile on her mouth wavered and fell away completely as she realized that while she had guessed right on Delilah coming to confront her, she hadn't counted on one simple thing.

Delilah wasn't alone.

Her eyes widened in shock as she saw the man standing just behind her daughter. A few phone calls had assured her that Sam Beaumont was at the hospital with his father. Fate for once was working in Louisa's favor because just before five, Junior had started running a fever and if Louisa knew anything about the Beaumonts, then she knew Sam would remain by his father's side until the doctor convinced him that Junior would be fine.

Had Sam accompanied Del, Louisa would have altered her plans accordingly. She could have dealt with this in a different matter and already had a few back ups in mind.

But she hadn't planned on Blake Mitchell. He wore no uniform but she could see the gold of his badge glinting from his belt and fear streaked through her. If he had his badge, did he also have his gun? Shaken, she fell back a step. Truly, she had to quell the urge to run.

But a Prescott never retreated. Right now, all she had to do was hide the gun. There would be another way to handle this.

₮

A chill raced down Blake's spine as he met Louisa's gaze. There was a manic look in those eyes, eyes so similar to Del's on the surface. Hell, *she* looked like Del, ageless beauty, class and intelligence. But Louisa was usually ice cold, cold enough that a lot of the guys like to joke that Sanders was either immune to frostbite or that he had a woman on the side that he kept damn quiet.

She was an icy piece of work, that was certain, but right now, all that ice was gone, melted into nothingness by something that made her eyes go wild. Almost insane.

Instinctively, he placed his body in front of Del's. Louisa's body stiffened.

"Miz Sanders," he said, keeping his voice soft and slow. "Del here needed to talk with you and your husband."

Louisa laughed but it was a false, high-pitched sound. "Delilah is welcome at any time." She retreated a step. Her right arm was behind her back and Blake reached out as Del tried to brush past him. Using his arm, he barred her way as he skimmed the grand foyer. There was an elaborate mirror to Louisa's right, hanging over a console table that gleamed from a recent dusting.

Her angle was wrong for him to see clearly, but the flash of something dark and matte was enough. Throwing himself backward, he grabbed Del and shoved her to the ground. He drew his weapon with one hand, the phone on his belt with the other.

Del lay on the ground, staring at him with stunned eyes. "Blake?"

He didn't answer, too busy dialing the phone and listening for the sound of movement inside the house. Del's eyes narrowed. Then there was a familiar sound—familiar to him, at least. He didn't know how long it took Del to figure it out but by the second gun shot, he could tell she had put it together.

"I need all available men to the Prescott manor," Blake said when dispatch came on the line. "ASAP. We've got shots fired."

Still crouched on the ground next to him, Del muttered, "Shots fired—by my *mother.*"

He gave her a narrow look and she clamped her lips shut. He tried to give a little more information to dispatch but another shot rang out, this one bursting through the wood and glass door frame just to his right. Wood and glass exploded and he ducked, throwing an arm up to protect his face.

"Stay down and head down the porch," he said, keeping his voice low.

The click of heels on polished hardwood came from the house and he ducked down, swatted Del on the butt and snapped, "Move!"

"Not without you," she returned, glaring at him over her shoulder.

"Right behind you, Deedee, now move."

She scrambled on her hands and knees and Blake backed along behind her, keeping his gun up and ready, one hand holding the butt of the gun and using the other hand to steady it. That long, white painted wrap around porch suddenly seemed about a mile or two in length. They were only halfway to the corner when Louisa stepped outside.

"Delilah, dear, you should really call before dropping in on somebody," Louisa said. Her voice sounded oddly disconnected and Blake saw next to no sign of sanity in her pale green eyes. She'd snapped, he realized. The woman had downright snapped.

Her voice pithy and sarcastic, Del replied, "Sorry, Mama. Didn't realize I needed an invitation to come inside my own house."

"Your house," Louisa said and this time, her voice shook. "Of course, your house. Because of your selfish bastard of a father. Should have been mine, Delilah. All of it. I *earned* it."

Del laughed, a brittle sound that seemed to echo in the silence. "You want it? Hey, that's fine. It's all yours."

Louisa sniffed and her face was once more all prim and proper, although her eyes, they were still wild and unbalanced. "It's too late now. You had to come home, didn't you, Delilah?"

"Louisa."

Blake placed his body between mother and daughter, drawing her eyes to him. He continued to back away. With his peripheral vision, he saw that they had reached the corner of the house and he heaved out a sigh, taking advantage of the cover and pressing his body to the wall. Still watching Louisa make her slow way towards them, he said to Del, "Keep moving. Get off the porch and get some place out of sight. Get to the car if you can."

"No fucking way."

"Del, damn it," he growled at her.

"I'm not leaving you."

He snarled. "Then will you at least get out of sight? I got enough to worry about."

A quick glance around the corner told him that while Louisa didn't appear to be in any hurry, she sure as hell managed to cover a lot of ground in a hurry. "Louisa, if you don't put the gun down, I'm going to have to shoot."

He heard Del's harsh intake of breath. Softly, he said, "I don't want to shoot you in front of your daughter, but I will."

Louisa laughed. It was a sane, almost logical sound and it scared him more than if she had broke into maniacal high-pitched cackles. Hell, he'd rather have the insane sound. It was damn disturbing to look into a face that looked completely sane, but stare into eyes that were completely *not*. "My darling daughter." Louisa sneered. "She's never been anything but trouble, from the time she was born. Her father actually expected me to breastfeed her—let some squalling, red-faced brat attach herself to me. He didn't like the idea of a nanny and refused to let me hire one. He wouldn't *pay* for one. He wanted *more* children. Didn't like to think of her being alone."

"Louisa, put the gun down. I'm not going to let you hurt her."

"She's taken everything else, Blake. My peace of mind, my home, my money. The only time she was ever useful was when she kept William out of my bed."

Fury pummeled him. His hand tensed and he could all but see himself squeezing the trigger. "How is shooting her going to get back your money? Your house? You don't think you'll get away with this, do you?"

"I would have. If you hadn't come," Louisa murmured, shaking her head. "I had it all planned out." She rounded the corner and Blake shifted so he could face her, and still check to see if Del had listened this time. She hadn't. Of course. She'd stood up and was staring at her mother with dark, angry eyes.

"I'm awful glad I didn't agree to that party of yours, Mama," Del said, her voice derisive.

"You never could do anything I asked," Louisa said. Then she gave Del an icy glare. "There is one thing I'd like—don't come to my funeral. I despise you."

I despise you.

So baldly, flatly stated. Del had always suspected that but still, hearing her mother say it hit her with the force of a backhand across her face and she stumbled back, reeling from the blow.

"I'm sorry for that, Mama."

"Sorry. Yes, you are sorry. Pathetic," Louisa said. Del watched as her mother smiled. "Darling. You really do need to do something about your hair. It's atrocious."

Then, with that smile still curling on her lips, Louisa lifted the gun.

Dread curdled inside Del but she couldn't move. Couldn't say anything. Even though she knew what was coming.

"Damn it, Louisa. Don't!" Blake shouted.

But she did anyway.

One final shot rang out. As Louisa's body crumpled to the floor, sirens rose up in the distance. Del staggered and if Blake hadn't wrapped his arms around her waist, she would have fallen to the floor.

Chapter Ten

I never could do what you wanted, Mama, Del thought as she stood over the grave, watching as the gleaming, pale pink coffin was lowered into the ground. It wasn't in the one adjacent to Del's father. Maybe it was petty of her, but she couldn't let her mother be buried next to a man she seemed to despise.

"Let's go, Del," Blake murmured, dipping his head to kiss her shoulder.

She shook her head. "No. Not yet."

Under her lashes, she saw her stepfather standing on the opposite side of the grave. He'd been admitted to the hospital the day her mother committed suicide and released the next day. A tox screen revealed that he had a high amount of sedatives in his blood, although Blake had grudgingly told her that William denied taking any medicine, just a glass of brandy that Louisa had given him.

The theory was that she had drugged him and planned to shoot him and blame it on Del. Whether she'd planned to kill Del and claim self-defense or make it look like suicide, they'd never know. An investigation of the grounds revealed that Louisa's black BMW wasn't on the premises and just last night, they'd tracked it down to a repair shop in Nashville. It had already been repaired and the only thing left was the paint job, but the pictures taken from when the car was brought in revealed front-end damage. They'd never know for certain, but it was entirely possible that Louisa had run Beaumont Junior off the road to keep him from speaking with Del.

William Sanders hadn't been much help but he did give a statement. According to that statement, Louisa had plans to kill Delilah but Sanders wasn't sure how or what she had planned beyond that.

Blake had a hard time saying Sanders's name without his face taking on a furious scowl. The protective way he hovered around her at the funeral and the visitation would have made her fall in love with him—if she wasn't already there. Sanders had attempted, one time, to approach Del and Blake had threatened bloody and very painful bodily harm if he tried it again.

Since then, Sanders had kept his distance. He'd moved out of the house and everything that he hadn't taken with him, Del had happily tossed into the huge trash bin that was sitting in the front yard. She'd meant it when she said she was gutting the wing where her step-father and her mother had lived. She was restoring it back to the way it had been before her dad died. If money and determination could do it, she was going to erase every sign that either of them had ever lived there.

Part of her did grieve for her mother, but more because she hadn't ever really had a mom—just a woman who carried her and gave birth to her. Louisa would have eaten her own young and admitting it hurt Del almost as much as hiding from it had.

Her hand shook as she held the pink rose over the casket and then let it fall. It landed on the gleaming surface and for one moment, Del stared it. She hadn't shed a tear in days. Del felt as though she should weep, but she remained dry eyed.

Men stood by silently, unobtrusive, but she knew they were waiting for everybody to leave so they could shovel dirt over the coffin. Holding out her shaking hand, she waited for Blake to take it.

Ready?" he asked, closing his fingers around hers and lifting them so he could kiss her knuckles.

But she wasn't. "I need to do something first." She slid a glance at William Sanders who was standing on the opposite side of the grave and graciously, politely thanking everybody who came to offer their condolences. He could be a charismatic man, her stepfather. She knew some people were muttering about how she'd kicked him out of the house, even though the truth had come out about how her mother and Sanders had been stealing her inheritance from her for years.

Part of her didn't want to care.

But unfortunately, it was the smaller part.

She needed to face him, just once, and prove to herself that he didn't have power over her, that he couldn't hurt her anymore. And—she wanted just a little bit of blood. Not figuratively, but she had to strike out at him. It was petty, it was stupid. And it was human nature. Wrong as it might be, she needed to do this.

"So I'll ask for forgiveness later," she muttered as the minister from First Christian of Prescott approached.

She smiled even though she wanted to cry and she thanked him for the lovely eulogy. It had been lovely. The minister had mentioned all the wonderful things Louisa had done for the community and how freely she had donated both time and money.

Although it had been done for the wrong reasons, Louisa had been big into charity. It was the fashionable, responsible thing to do. Del already had Sam looking into her mother's responsibilities and she intended to make sure each and every obligation was met. Unlike her mother, Del believed that people who had a great deal should give out of gratitude, not to look good socially.

Lincoln Vanderhall continued to speak to her, in the soft, consoling way only a minister could manage, his hands cupping hers and she forced herself to smile and nod and answer questions when all she wanted was some peace and quiet. Finally, she tugged her hand away and said, "If you don't mind, I'm worn out."

She left him behind her while he murmured his understanding and she circled around the grave. The spikes of her heels dug into the earth and she navigated the uneven ground like she hadn't spent even a day out of the sexy, ridiculous shoes that society pushed on females.

"Del."

Blake laid a hand on her shoulder and she paused,

looked back at him. "I need to do this," she said softly. Reaching up, she covered his hand with hers and added, "And I need you with me."

"Do I get to kill him?"

Sighing, Del glanced at the grave. "I think there's been enough death for a while."

His mouth twisted in a grimace and he ran his hands up and down her arms. "Sorry, baby." Then he smiled hopefully. "Can I hurt him? Or hold him while you do it?"

Del chuckled. Reaching up, she caught one of his hands and linked their fingers. "Oh, don't worry. I'm going to do something that will hurt him." She eyed the man standing behind Sanders. He was older, graying and distinguished. He also had two suited men standing at his shoulder, another waiting on the path, and two more standing by the black limo at the end of the path.

She wasn't overly interested in following politics but she recognized this man. "That's Senator Watkins isn't it?"

"Yeah," Blake said with a frown. "Voted for the guy last election. Won't do it again, though. There's a rumor floating around that he wants to groom your stepdad for a dip into politics. So obviously his ability to judge character sucks."

Del's smile widened. "Really."

If Williams Sanders had any real sense, the smile on Del's face would have warned him, Blake figured. He walked at her side and had to bite back a smile as she pulled her shoulders back and her eyes took on a wicked gleam. "Hello, William," she said, placing her body between him and the grave.

William glanced from her to Blake. His lids flickered a little and he quickly looked back at Del. Apparently the man didn't like something he saw on Blake's face. *Can't imagine what*, Blake thought as he opened and close one hand, imagined how it would feel to slam his fist into William's face. Repeatedly.

"Delilah. You did wonderful by your mother. She'd be proud."

Del snorted. "Actually, she told me she didn't want me at her funeral." She cocked her head and her hair, dark, thick and straight, fell over one shoulder. "Either the years have been good to you or you've got one hell of a plastic surgeon."

A ruddy flush stained his cheeks red but he didn't respond. "You're as beautiful as your mother, but then, you always were. You were a beautiful girl and you're a beautiful woman. I've missed seeing you."

Oh. Totally wrong *thing to say*, Del thought, her entire body tensing. *Beautiful girl. My pretty little slut.* The words circled through her head, but instead of reeling from nausea and fear, she went stiff with anger. Her hand clenched into a fist and she wanted to hit him. But the physical pain wouldn't ruin him. After all, it hadn't ruined her.

With a sugary sweet smile, she said, "So who did you rape after I left? Couldn't have been Mama."

William's spine went ramrod straight, like somebody

has shoved a poker up his ass. His mouth twisted and his face went a florid shade of red. Behind him, the Senator's lids flickered. He glanced at one of the black suits who stood at his side and then back at Del.

"Delilah, I know you're upset—"

He reached out but before he could touch her, Blake caught his wrist. Del watched as Blake squeezed, squeezed so hard his knuckles went white and William's hand started to go purple in Blake's grasp. "Don't touch her, William. Remember what I told you would happen."

William jerked back and slowly, Blake let go. Del grinned at the look of fear on William's face. Then her smile faded. "Upset?" she repeated softly. "Yeah, seeing my mother kill herself in front of me was upsetting. Hearing her say that she despised me was upsetting. But no more upsetting than knowing she didn't care how often you raped me as long as you left her alone."

His face twisted in a sneer and she could see it in his eyes, how much he wanted to hurt her. He wouldn't, though. Not here. Keeping her voice quiet, she said, "You damn near destroyed my life, *Father*. But I'm not going to let you affect it any more. You're dead to me." Then she shifted her gaze to the man waiting just behind Sanders, looking like he wanted to be any where but here. "The summer I was sixteen, this man spent two months raping me, beating me. My mother knew and she didn't care. I don't know which monster is worse, him or her. But now you know what he is. Do you really want to put somebody like him in office?"

"Ahh. No. No, madam, I do not." Senator Watkins glanced at his men and then gave Del a short nod.

"Paul—"

The Senator looked back at Sanders for a brief moment. His mouth tightened in a flat line and shook his head. Saying nothing, he walked away.

When Sanders looked back at her, Del smirked. "Not the immediate satisfaction I'd get from seeing Blake beat you bloody, but in the long run? A lot more satisfying. Stay away from me from here on out. Otherwise, the next time I discuss this, it's going to be in a much more public venue."

℥

"You're not going to pass out on me, are you?" Blake asked lightly, but he wasn't joking. Not exactly. Del sat sideways in the front seat of his cruiser, her feet still on the dusty gravel, her arms wrapped protectively around her middle. She rocked back and forth, slow, subtle rhythm that he doubted she was even aware of. Her eyes were what bothered him the most though. Her pale green eyes were glassy and unfocused. When she looked at him, he didn't think she really saw him.

He crouched in front of her and reached out, taking her hands. They were cold. Her lips looked bloodless. "Come on, Del. Say something."

She opened her mouth but no words came out. Her breaths came in fast, erratic pants and Blake reached up, cupped the back of her neck and forced her head down. "Calm down, Del. Take a deep breath, baby. Come on...that's it. Breathe for me. Slow...slow..."

Voice muffled, Del said, "Let me up."

"Slow," he warned her again as she went to straighten up. She still looked pale, but that white, pinched look to her mouth had faded. "You steady?"

"I don't know." Her gaze shifted to the left and Blake didn't even have to turn around to know whom she had seen. "I can't believe I just did that."

Linking their fingers, he remained still and waited.

She laughed, but it wasn't a humorous sound. It was bitter and ugly and it hurt his heart to hear it. "You know, I've only told four people what he did to me. Mama—and she didn't believe me. You, Manda—and Joely."

"Who is Joely?"

A sad, bittersweet smile curved her lips. "My guardian angel." Her gaze met his and she said quietly, "Joely pulled me out of hell. I knew I was walking a bad road. There were different people who tried to help, but I wouldn't listen to them. Joely wouldn't let me *not* listen. She saved my life."

"When can I meet her so I can say thanks?"

Tears welled in her eyes but she blinked them back. "She's dead. Died of cancer a year ago." Taking a deep, shaky breath, she murmured, "Four people. And then I go and blurt it out in front of a Senator and his bodyguards."

He lifted her hand and kissed the back of it. "Do you

regret it?"

"I don't know. Some, maybe." Her mouth quirked in a grin. "But the look on William's face..."

Laughing softly, Blake said, "Oh, that was priceless. Almost as good as if I had pounded him a few times." The limo was long gone from their sight, but they both remembered the faint look of disgust that Senator Watkins had shot at Sanders before climbing into his car. "He's ruined, you know. Watkins won't say anything about this, but without the Senator's support, Sanders doesn't stand a chance in politics. Word will get around that Sanders is a bad bet. This mess with your mother, it isn't going to help. People are already talking about the money they stole from you."

A grimace twisted her soft mouth. "Yeah, I know. A few of people think I'm being heartless, tossing him out like that, money or not."

With a shake of his head, Blake assured her, "That will pass. He's a rich man, but not a liked one. Not a respected one. It's not really much justice, though, is it?"

Del lifted up a hand and laid it against his cheek. "I don't need justice, Blake. I just needed to accept it—and figure out how to move on with my life."

"And have you figured that out?"

She smiled again, but this one wasn't bleak, bitter or sad. Instead, she looked thoughtful, hopeful even. Leaning in, she kissed him softly and murmured against his lips, "Working on it."

"Hmmmm." He nibbled on her lower lip. "I'd be happy

to help you figure it out if you want." Sucking her lip into his mouth, he bit soft and gentle and then stroked her with his tongue.

The sound of her breath catching in her throat sent a surge of heat through him. Reluctantly, he pulled back and rested his brow against hers. "You ready to go?"

Lifting her head, she looked around. Her gaze drifted to an area of the cemetery off to the south. Blake followed her gaze. "I can walk you over there, if you want," he offered.

But Del just shook her head. "I've had about as much of this place as I can take for the day. Not today." She closed her eyes and sat there for a minute, still as death. Then she looked back at him and gave him a watery smile. This time, when the tears welled in her eyes, she didn't try to hold them back. "Daddy would understand, I think. He never liked coming here much to visit his mama after she died. Always said life was for living, not for crying over those who've already passed."

Pushing her dark, silky hair back from her face, Blake leaned in and kissed her brow. He breathed in the warm, sweet scent of her body, letting it flood his system. The heat came, but it wasn't just heat.

Blake hadn't been the one to leave home twelve years ago, but all the same, losing her, it had cut him adrift. In that moment, with the warmth of the August sun shining down on them as they stood in a stone garden surrounded by the memory of death, he realized he felt like he'd come home too.

"Come on." He rubbed his lips against hers and murmured, "Let's get out of here."

Nearly forty minutes later, the hot summer wind blowing in through the open windows of the cruiser, Blake turned down the long gravel road that would lead to the lake house. He'd asked her where she wanted to go and she'd said, "Any place but the Manor. I'm not up for attending the wake, Blake." Since then, she'd stared out the window in silence but as he sped up, she glanced over at him. "I reckon half the town is going to think I'm doing something unforgivable, cutting out on my mother's wake."

He shook his head and reached over, curving his hand over the back of her neck and squeezing gently. "Don't you worry about them. Manda's there and Vance. They'll handle it. Considering how it happened, I can imagine most of them would understand why you aren't ready to go back to the Manor."

"I'm going to redecorate. Put the Manor back to the way it was before Mama married him. I want it the way it was back when Daddy was alive." She smirked, looking just a little less lost. "I certainly have the money for it now, don't I?"

"How are you going to do that working in Cincinnati?"

Sliding a look at him, she murmured, "My, that was subtle." Then she leaned her head back against the seat and closed her eyes. "I'm turning in my notice. Moving back here."

A minute passed before he trusted himself to respond.

"They going to be okay with you leaving?"

A faint smile curved her lips. "At first? Maybe not. They need me...Or rather, they need somebody there who will do what I was doing, for the salary I received. But..." Her voice trailed off.

He glanced at her and saw that faint smile had widened into a pleased grin. "I've got more money now than I know what to do with. They could use some of it. Hell, they could use a *lot*. So I'm going to see what I can do about that. Maybe they can get a decent staff in there. They do good things. With some money, with the right resources...they could do more."

Looking at him, she shrugged. "Believe me, once I talk to my boss, he'll be more than happy with the trade." Then she sighed and turned her head to look out the window. "This is home, Blake. Always has been. I think it's time I come back."

Blake said nothing. He couldn't. He wanted to, but he wasn't so sure he could speak around the knot in his throat. Even if he could, he had absolutely no idea what he'd say. The relief inside him, it had made him, blind, deaf and dumb to anything, to everything. Except one thing.

Touching her. Blake just had to touch her. The lake house was still out of sight, lost among the trees, although he could make out the water, the sun shining down on it and glinting like diamonds. Pulling off the road, he put the car into park and then reached for her. Fumbling with her seat belt, he swore as the damn thing resisted him, all but tangling under his hands as he jerked at it. Del laughed softly and reached down, brushing his hands aside and releasing the belt. She came to him, coming across the console and cuddling against his chest.

Fisting a hand in her hair, he angled her head back, stared into her pale eyes. "You coming back just because you miss home?" he asked, his voice rusty.

Lowering her lashes over her eyes, she shrugged. "I have missed home."

The adrenaline that had been coursing through his veins drained out and his heart dropped into his stomach like a lead weight. *Of course she missed home.* Time splintered around him and he wondered if he could do this. If she came home but decided that she wasn't ready to try it with him after all, it was going to kill him.

Hell, he felt half dead inside already.

Her hand cupped his cheek and he shifted his gaze back to hers. She was smiling again, a secretive smile that only a female could manage—one that was designed just to drive men crazy. "Maybe I should also tell you that this place wouldn't be home, if you weren't here."

Just like that, his life realigned itself. "So what are you coming back for? Home? Me?"

Squirming around, she wiggled and shifted, working her long, skinny skirt up so she could put a knee on either side of his hips. The steering wheel was at her back and it was a tight fit—a perfect fit, as far as he was concerned because she was pressed close and snug to his body. "You are home, Blake. Much as I missed Prescott, much as I missed Manda and my friends and the lake, you're what I thought of when I thought of home." She kissed him, using her tongue and her teeth, sliding her hands up his back over his neck. She tugged off the black cloth he had covering his bare scalp, stroking him gently.

Her hips moved in desperate circles and Blake rested his hands on her thighs, feeling the softness and the strength there. The heat of her sex was a silken, sweet promise and his hips surged upward to meet that frenzied rocking. Sliding his hands up her skirt, he worked his hands under her panties and tried to tug them off. She arched back to help him and ending up honking the horn.

They stilled and then looked at each other and laughed. Del glanced over his shoulder and murmured, "You think we'd get arrested if we did it in the back of the cruiser?"

Grinning, he pulled her mouth down to meet his. "Maybe. But my girlfriend's loaded. She can bail us out."

Laughing, they fought their way out of the car, tripping over each other, tangled up and so focused on the other, the entire Sheriff's department could have surrounded them and they probably wouldn't have noticed. He grasped the handle of the back door and jerked on it, fumbled it open and fell into the back, pulling her with him. The back door was wide open, but neither of cared enough to notice.

Sliding his hands under the hem of her skirt, Blake shoved it to her waist. Del dipped her head and kissed his throat above the starched collar of the pale gray Armani shirt, licking at him like a kitten.

He growled and grabbed her underwear, jerking. The fragile silk gave under his hands and fell away in scraps. While her fingers busily worked to loosen his tie, he fumbled between them for his belt and zipper. Finally, he freed himself and a harsh breath hissed out of him as she rubbed against him, cuddling her silky wet heat against him.

Laughter faded as she straightened on top of him and stared down at him. Blake cupped her face in his hand, rubbed his thumb across her lower lip. "I love you," he whispered.

Turning her head, she kissed his hand. "I love you too." Her lids drooped low and she rocked against him again. The silken friction had him arching off the back seat of the car. Grasping her hip with his free hand, he held her steady as he pressed close to her. "I'm a mess, though, Blake," she whispered as he urged her down.

Wrapping his arm around her waist, he pushed inside her. "Who isn't?" He bit down on her chin. "Marry me."

Tears came to her eyes. Her spine bowed as he forged on, relentless. He didn't stop until he was buried hilt deep in her pussy and then he cupped her face in his hands. Circling his hips, he thrust inside her slow and steady. "Marry me, Del."

She gasped, lids fluttering over her eyes as he stroked deep. "You sure you want to take a chance on me, Blake? I still don't always know which way is up."

Pushing her hair back, he tugged her mouth down until he could cover it with his. "Don't worry. I'm good with directions. Just say you'll marry me."

Del whimpered and rocked against him. Straightening slowly, she watched him and started to move, lazy movements that set his blood to simmering. She tightened around him, satin slick, and sweet. Blake stared at her from under his lashes. She hadn't answered him but he was content to wait, for now. Her skirt was shoved up to her waist, baring long, strong thighs, sleekly curved and smooth. The muscles flexed as her knees tightened around his hips, riding him. The short-waisted, black suit jacket matched the skirt perfectly. It was prim and demure and hid too damn much of her body.

He freed the buttons carefully, not tearing at them the way he wanted. When the last button was freed, he pushed it open but left it hanging on her shoulders. There was a strand of creamy pearls around her throat and they gleamed. A black bra cupped her breasts and under the sheer lace, he could see the pink of her nipples.

"You're so fucking pretty," he muttered. "So damn beautiful..."

As soon as he said it, he wished he could yank it back. He saw her eyes darken, watched as the heat was replaced by ice. But he couldn't take it back, couldn't turn back the clock. But he also couldn't let go of her as she shoved against him. Easing up, he wrapped a hand around her waist, held her close. "Beautiful isn't an ugly word, Del. You don't want to let him win, then you can't keep letting things like this pull you back," he whispered, cupping her face and forcing her to look at him.

Her eyes open wide, she stared at him. Her entire body trembled, like a leaf blowing in the wind. Soothingly, he kissed her lips, her cheek, nuzzled her neck. "You are beautiful. You're soft, you're sexy...you're the woman I've loved my entire life."

"Blake..." Her voice was thick with tears and he eased back, staring into her eyes.

"Shhh..." he whispered. "Close your eyes...listen to me, to my voice...feel my hands. You're beautiful, Del. You make my heart hurt just to look at you..." Gently, he slid his hand down the center of her body, pausing to cup her breast, then circle his index finger around her navel.

When she didn't pull away, he went lower and continued to whisper to her. "You're beautiful..." Her lids lifted up and he forced himself to smile, although he ached with fury, ached with need, ached with love. "It's not a dirty word, Del. It's just a word...you decide how to take it."

"Beautiful," he repeated, stroking lower, lower, lower so he could comb through the blonde curls that covered her pussy. As he touched her clit, he stared at her, watching her eyes widen, her pupils flare. A ragged moan escaped her and her sex went tight around his cock. Blake wondered that he just didn't explode under the heat and silk.

"Beautiful..." This time it was forced out through gritted teeth as he held his climax back by a thread. Jaw clenched, eyes closed so the sexy sight of her half-clothed and riding him didn't send him over. With quick, sure strokes, he caressed her clit and she keened, screaming out his name. Her nails dug into his shirt as she fisted her hands.

She started to come. Desperate for her, he fisted a hand in her hair and pulled her down to meet his mouth. She screamed and he swallowed the sound down, growling in triumph.

"Beautiful," he growled, tearing his mouth from hers to say it once. The second time, he shouted it as his orgasm slammed into him. *Mine,* he thought. *Mine again, and this time, I won't let you go.*

Blake didn't realize he'd spoken out loud until after the storm passed and she sagged against him. "You won't have to, Blake. I'm done running and I'm not going anywhere."

About the Author

To learn more about Shiloh Walker, please visit
http://shilohwalker.com or

http://shilohwalker.wordpress.com.

Send an email to Shiloh Walker at
Shiloh_@shilohwalker.com or join her Yahoo! group to
join in the fun with other readers as well as Shiloh
http://groups.yahoo.com/group/SHI_nenigans.

*Someone wants a secret to stay buried—even
if it means murder.*

For the Love of Jazz
© 2007 Shiloh Walker

Since waking up in a hospital at age eighteen, accused of driving the car that killed his best friend, Jazz McNeil has lived with a guilty heart. Now, more than a decade later, he has returned to his hometown to raise his daughter and to uncover the truth about what happened that fateful summer. And gaze into the eyes of the girl whose life he shattered.

Though Anne-Marie Kincaid was told that Jazz was responsible for her brother's death all those years ago, she has never quite believed it. The facts don't quite fit; they never did. All she knows is, she still feels loved and safe when she's with Jazz, and that he misses her brother just as much as she.

And since he returned home, people have started dying.

Available now in ebook and print from Samhain Publishing.

All small towns have secrets. This one could be deadly

The Seduction of Shamus O'Rourke
© 2007 N.J. Walters
Book 4 of Jamesville.

After her father's death, Cyndi Marks returns to Jamesville, determined to settle here and lay the ghosts of years ago to rest once and for all. But the past has a way of catching up—and hanging on.

When her car breaks down outside of town, a handsome stranger stops to help. He intrigues and attracts her, but then she discovers who he is.

Shamus O'Rourke enjoys his job, his family and small town living. What he's missing is someone with whom to share it. Immediately drawn to Cyndi, he is determined to get closer to her, even as he senses her pulling away.

But not everyone in Jamesville is happy to see Cyndi. People are hiding secrets. Secrets they would kill to protect. When violence erupts in her home, Cyndi turns to the only person in town she can trust—Shamus.

In a situation where family loyalties are strained, Cyndi's life is threatened and everyone is a suspect, will their emerging love survive?

Available now in ebook and print from Samhain Publishing.

hot stuff

Discover Samhain!

THE HOTTEST NEW PUBLISHER ON THE PLANET

Romance, fantasy, mystery, thriller, mainstream and more—Samhain has more selection, hotter authors, and everything's available in both ebook and print.

Pick your favorite, sit back, and enjoy the ride! Hot stuff indeed.

WWW.SAMHAINPUBLISHING.COM

GET IT NOW

MyBookStoreAndMore.com

GREAT EBOOKS, GREAT DEALS . . . AND MORE!

Don't wait to run to the bookstore down the street, or
waste time shopping online at one of the "big boys." Now,
all your favorite Samhain authors are all in one place—at
MyBookStoreAndMore.com. Stop by today and discover
great deals on Samhain—and a whole lot more!

WWW.SAMHAINPUBLISHING.COM

Printed in the United States
144197LV00003B/2/P